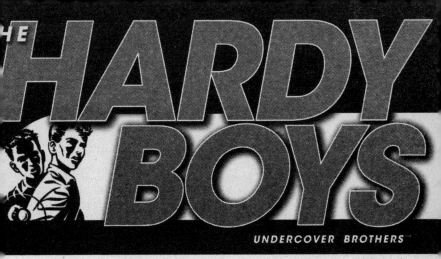

THE HARDY BOYS

BOYS

UNDERCOVER BROTHERS

#20 Feeding Frenzy

FRANKLIN W. DIXON

Aladdin Paperbacks
New York   London   Toronto   Sydney

❧ ALADDIN PAPERBACKS

An imprint of Simon & Schuster Children's Publishing Division

1230 Avenue of the Americas, New York, NY 10020

Copyright © 2008 by Simon & Schuster, Inc.

All rights reserved, including the right of reproduction in whole or in part in any form.

THE HARDY BOYS MYSTERY STORIES and HARDY BOYS UNDER-COVER BROTHERS are registered trademarks of Simon & Schuster, Inc.

ALADDIN PAPERBACKS and related logo are registered trademarks of Simon & Schuster, Inc.

Designed by Lisa Vega

The text of this book was set in Aldine 401 BT.

Manufactured in the United States of America

First Aladdin Paperbacks edition January 2008

10 9 8 7 6 5 4 3

Library of Congress Control Number 2007932268

ISBN-13: 978-1-4169-5499-6

ISBN-10: 1-4169-5499-6

TABLE OF CONTENTS

1.
Fight Fire with Fire

Joe and I struggled to carry Barry Egan's limp body through the forest. "We should have thought about how heavy he was before we knocked him out," Joe said.

"What's this 'we'?" I asked. I tightened my grip on Barry's legs.

"You know I had to do it," said Joe. "He was one second away from lighting the match. With the wind like it is today, the whole forest could have gone up."

"You're right," I agreed.

"And I didn't hit him that hard," Joe added. "He should be coming to in a minute. Then he can walk on his own two feet."

"But carrying him is such good exercise," I

protested. "I can almost feel my biceps getting—"

A blast of light exploded to my left. I jerked my head toward it. And it was like somebody had turned on a gas jet. That's how fast the wildfire seemed to have started. The instructors in our teen firefighting course had told us it could be like this, but I'd never fully wrapped my head around the concept.

"Barry must have gotten a fire started before we tracked him down." Joe stared at the blaze, wide-eyed.

"We're uphill from it . . . ," I began.

"That means it's going to be traveling toward us," Joe finished for me. "There's no way we're going to be able to outrun it."

That had been drilled into our heads. A person can't outrun a forest fire. It could move at more than fourteen miles an hour under the right conditions. And the conditions out here were right. We might as well have been standing in a pile of kindling. And there was a breeze. A breeze coming in our direction.

"Come on. This way." I tightened my grip on Barry's legs and took a step to the right.

Joe didn't move. "Are you insane? That pretty red and orange stuff back there—that's the fire. That's where the heat is coming from. We don't want to be moving toward it."

"We passed a little clearing not that far back," I

explained. "We can create a safety zone. I don't think there's any other way we're going to make it."

"Okay. Now that I know what you're thinking, okay. Not happy, but on board," said Joe. "Let's move."

Where is it? Where is it? I thought, scanning the woods in front of me for the clearing. If it was much farther, I'd made a serious miscalculation. The heat from the fire already felt like it was singeing off a layer of my body.

"Do you see it?" Joe asked. He was walking backward with his end of Barry.

"Not yet. Wait. Yeah. We just have to veer left a little," I answered. The relief felt as good as dumping a bottle of water over my head. "Let's leave Barry here until we have the space ready," I said when we were about ten feet away from the clearing.

We lowered Barry to the ground. Joe immediately started searching our captive's pockets. "An arsonist is definitely going to have some good fire-starting materials on him. Matches." He tossed the book to me. "And . . . score! Lighter fluid." He held up a small metal can.

Together we walked over to the clearing. "In class they said we'd need to burn out an area about as big as the room we were in that day," I said.

"Right." Joe moved to the middle of the clearing,

the dry grass crunching under his feet. I checked the wildfire's progress as he began squirting the lighter fluid over a wide area. The fire was closer. I could hear panicked animals racing away from it. But I thought we still had enough time.

"Whaas?" Barry mumbled. He swallowed hard. Concentrated. "What's goin' on?"

I turned around and saw him struggling to sit up. "You must be happy. This is the biggest one you've managed to start yet."

Barry squinted at the fire and looked almost proud of himself. "Our crew will be able to help stop it. Then firefighters will need us, and they'll see we aren't just cupcakes. That we can handle the real deal and that we deserve the real jobs. Not just fake fires at summer camp."

He rubbed the back of his head. "What happened to me?"

"Joe knocked you out," I told him. "But obviously not soon enough. People might die out here today, Barry. *We* might die out here. Then you'll never get your real job. Not that you will anyway. Arsonists don't get hired as firefighters."

"I used up all the fluid," Joe called over to me.

"Okay, let's light her up," I answered as I headed over to him. "You stay there," I ordered Barry over my shoulder.

I waited until Joe was out of the area he'd dowsed with the lighter fluid, then I lit a match and flicked it inside. Joe and I backed up fast. With a *whomp* the grass in the middle of the clearing ignited.

"Setting a fire to survive a fire." Joe shook his head. "It still seems wrong."

"But fire needs fuel to burn. That fuel will be gone fast." I noticed the flames were already not quite as high. "When the wildfire hits here, it will have to go around this spot, because there's not going to be anything for it to feed on."

"It's coming fast," Joe said.

"The grass is burning fast too. It's going to be okay," I answered.

Barry shoved himself to his feet. He stared around, like he was thinking about running.

"If you want to stay alive, you better stay here," Joe told him. He pulled off his shirt. "Looks like the fire's pretty much died out in the safe zone." He walked over and stared beating at the last flickering flames with his shirt.

I took mine off and helped him. "Get in here," I ordered Barry.

He hesitated, then walked over to the blackened patch of earth and stepped inside. I pulled a bottle of water out of my backpack, soaked part of my shirt, and passed the bottle to Joe. He did the same, then handed the bottle to Barry.

"We should get low," Joe said, then pressed his wet shirt over his nose and mouth and hunkered down on the ground, his head against his knees.

I got in the same position, feeling the heat of the ground soaking into the soles of my hiking boots. I concentrated on taking even breaths. I could taste the smoke, even through the wet cloth of my shirt. And I could feel the hair on my arms cracking from the heat.

The roar of the fire filled my ears. I couldn't believe my skin wasn't bubbling.

Something soft brushed against me. A deer? I didn't look up to see. I kept my head down. And I breathed.

Until I realized that the deafening sound of the flames had gotten a little quieter. Slowly I straightened up and took in the changed world around me. Our small patch of charred earth had become a huge, black wasteland. The fire had passed through, taking everything in its path.

A new sound cut through the air. "Chopper," Joe called.

"Firefighters," I answered. I turned to Barry. "I think you found a way to make a big impression on them."

2.

The Worst Christmas Present Ever

I needed an escape route. Now. I could hear thudding footfalls right behind me. And I could practically smell the stinky breath of—

Wham!

Two hands drove into my back, which was still feeling charbroiled, by the way. And two seconds later, I was eating grass on my front lawn. "I thought we were playing touch. That was more like slam," I muttered.

Brian Conrad dropped to his knees and got right in my face. "Aww, did I hurt poor li'l Joe?" he crooned, blasting me with the odor of Cool Ranch Doritos mixed with extreme halitosis.

"Poor li'l Joe is just fine," I answered. But I couldn't help giving a little grunt of pain as I stood

7

up. Brian grinned. He'd heard my grunt and he'd enjoyed it. Dillweed.

Frank and I got in a huddle with Chet Morton, the other guy on our team. Chet's not exactly what you would call athletic. He's exactly what you would call a couch potato. Usually my brother and I could carry him in a game of touch football. But today, Frank and I were both on the injured list. And our team was getting its behind kicked.

"Okay, here's what we do," Frank said, quarterbacking. "I hike to Joe. Joe, you hand it off to Chet and haul for the goal line. Chet, hang back, keep the ball close, and let everyone go after Joe. Then make your move."

"Got it." I tossed the ball to Frank, then got into position behind him. He leaned over, kind of slowly. Charbroiled bodies don't really like to bend.

"What's wrong? Your pantyhose bunching up on you?" Greg Neemy called out.

I laughed, because, (1) Greg Neemy isn't a jerk like Brian, and (2) stuff like that is pretty much always funny when it's said about your brother and not about you.

Frank hiked the ball to me. I did a slick handoff to Chet and tore down the lawn like my feet were on fire and there was a lake right across the goal line. By the thundering sounds behind me, I'd picked up at least two of the three guys on the other team. Excellent.

Excellent until a foot caught me in the back of my knee. *Whomp!* And yes, I was eating grass again. I'd eaten more grass during this game than a dog with a stomachache!

"You like my new technique?" asked Brian as I heaved myself to my feet with, yes, a grunt. "Foot-tag football."

"One problem. You foot-tagged the wrong guy," I told him.

Before Brian could get out a word, Chet bounced the football off the driveway and started into his victory dance. You know how when you were little and you had to go to the bathroom but you didn't want to stop playing, so you just kind of squirmed and wiggled around a lot? That's basically Chet's touchdown dance. Sadly, he uses almost the same moves when he attempts to dance with a girl.

"We should head back inside," Frank called. "We don't want to miss any of the real game."

"Yeah, halftime should be almost over," Mark Smallwood, the third guy on Brian's team, agreed. "And I don't want to miss one second of the Seahawks' road to the Super Bowl." He said that "road to the Super Bowl" part in a sports announcer voice, complete with mike reverb.

You have to cut Mark some slack. He grew up in Seattle. All the rain leaked into his ears and made his gray matter moldy. He really isn't able to comprehend that the Jets are now, always will be, always have been, the best football team in existence.

Even if they are already out of the play-offs.

Frank led the way back inside to the living room. "Wimps! Wimps! Wimps!" our parrot, Playback, called from the kitchen as we walked by.

"Smart bird. He knows his owners," Brian commented as he flopped down on the couch.

Why is this guy in my house eating my Doritos? I thought, watching Brian get his snout in the tortilla chips again.

Answer: because Frank and I were friends with Mark. And somehow Mark was friends with Brian. Maybe it was another side effect of the Seattle brain mold.

Frank clicked on the TV. "Good, it hasn't started back up," said Mark. He took a seat on the floor, focusing all his attention on the screen.

I grabbed a piece of floor next to him. I also grabbed the bowl of Doritos off the coffee table. Hey, it was my house. Well, my parents'. And I was getting my share. I jammed as many into my

10

mouth as I could fit. The sharp edges of the triangles cut into my cheeks, and some of the cool ranch felt like it was traveling up my nose instead of down my throat. I kept on chewin'.

"Joe, you're the one who should be in that contest," Chet said.

"Thaa whaa?" I mumbled through the glob of goop in my mouth. I was still working on swallowing.

"The Football Franks Hot Dog Eating Contest on Super Bowl Sunday," Frank explained, nodding toward the screen.

Oh, right. I'd seen the commercial a bunch of times. It had been running during all the play-off games. This new hot dog company was having an eating contest. They were going to pay the winner five hundred dollars an inch for every inch of hot dog they managed to shove down during the halftime of the Super Bowl.

"How much do you think the winner will get?" asked Greg.

"Halftime is how long, you think?" Frank said. I could almost hear the calculator in his head firing up.

"Regular game halftimes are twelve minutes. Superbowl halfs are usually double that," Mark answered.

"We need to take off a little time for start-up and wrap-up. They're going to announce the winner on TV right there at halftime, so they'll need a few minutes to figure that out. Let's say, ballpark, twenty minutes for the contest," said Frank.

"Football stadium," Chet corrected.

"What?" I asked. I could say it clearly, because I'd swallowed all my Doritos.

"Football stadium, not ballpark," Chet explained.

I groaned. At least it wasn't a groan of physical pain this time. Just very bad joke pain.

"And how many hot dogs do you think you can eat in a minute?" Frank continued, not bothering to comment on Chet's comment.

"They're thirteen inches. That's why they're paying by the inch," said Greg. "They want to play up how they're an inch longer than regular hot dogs."

"I bet I could eat seven a minute," Brian told the group.

"Come on," I protested.

"What? That's just a little more than one every ten seconds," Brian shot back.

"I like hot dogs, okay?" I told him. "And I can eat me some hot dogs. I bet I could eat even twelve in a minute. One every five seconds. But not for the whole halftime. Nobody could keep that pace up for twenty minutes straight."

"If you tried it, you'd have to subtract at least some puking minutes," Mark agreed.

"All right. Let's say an average of three hot dogs a minute over the whole twenty," Frank said. "That's sixty hot dogs, so seven hundred eighty inches of hot dog, at five hundred dollars an inch." He closed his eyes for a second, then opened them when he had the answer. "Three hundred and ninety thou."

Greg let out a long whistle.

"That's if you're a loser who can only eat three hot dogs a minute," Brian muttered.

"You can only use the cash for college, though," said Mark. "The contest is just for teenagers, so of course the powers that be want to make sure the money is used responsibly."

"Yeah, and Mark was hoping to buy the Seahawks so he could make them play in his front yard every day," Greg joked.

"The game should be back on any minute," Mark reminded us. "When it starts, I need—"

"Complete silence," the rest of us answered together. As if you could watch football in silence.

"It's so the Hawks can receive my brainwaves," Mark explained. "They need to feel me cheering them on, even though I'm not there in person. It's a—"

He was interrupted by the doorbell.

"You better disconnect that," said Greg as I stood up to answer it. "The electrical impulses would probably really mess up Mark's brain waves. Maybe you should shut off the lights, too," he called after me. "And the TV, except then, hey, we wouldn't be able to watch the game at all!"

I opened the front door, the sounds of what Aunt Trudy would call "some silliness" starting up in the living room behind me.

Nobody was there. Weird.

I started to shut the door, when a flash of red and silver caught my eye. A large Christmas present sat at my feet. I picked it up. The "To" part of the tag read "Frank and Joe Hardy." The "From" part of the tag was blank.

Also weird.

Also, also weird? Christmas was almost a month ago.

Which made me think this wasn't a Christmas present at all. I was thinking Joe and I had just gotten another ATAC mission, even though we'd just wrapped up the teen arsonist case for American Teens Against Crime.

I decided to hustle the box upstairs and open it.

I didn't want to have to come up with any explanations for Brian and crew. Plus, if it turned out to be an actual present, I'd get first dibs.

I started for the stairs. "Hey, you got a present!" Greg said as he headed for the bathroom. "Open it up. Maybe it's cookies."

"I was just going to stick it in my room for now," I told him. "The game's about to start and everything."

"Hey, you guys. Joe just got a present of probably edible stuff and he's not sharing," Greg announced loudly.

"I'm ashamed of you, Joe Hardy!" Chet called from the living room. "Don't you remember what we learned in first grade about sharing? Get in here."

"Thanks," I muttered to Greg. He grinned at me. "I'm coming, I'm coming!" I yelled back to Chet. It was pointless to try to get the package up to my room now. One of my so-called friends would just tackle me and rip it open. If I kept control of the box, I'd at least keep some control of the situation.

"It's for both of us," I told Frank as I walked back into the living room.

I started to unwrap the present, but Frank wrestled it out of my hands. He carefully pulled up the tape and slid off the paper. Yes, he's one of those. And you thought they were all old ladies, didn't you? It's okay to admit it.

 FRANK

Frank here. Anyone concerned about the environment—which should be everyone, since the environment is where we live—recycles wrapping paper by saving it for future gifts.

 JOE

Get out of here. This is my part. And how old-lady was that? "Since the environment is where we live." Come on. It's true, but come on.

"Are you an old woman or what?" Brian demanded.

I just agreed with Brian Conrad. That is the first sign of the apocalypse. You'd better head for your basement. I hope you have lots of canned food and bottled water.

Frank ignored him. I leaned over his shoulder as he pulled off the lid. He moved the tissue paper covering the contents aside.

I wasn't *too* worried, because our ATAC missions come on game cartridges, so the guys shouldn't get suspicious if that's who the package was from. Although sometimes cash and other supplies came with the cartridge.

It'll be okay, I told myself. *We'll be able to come up with a decent explanation for whatever they see.*

3.

Death in the Center Ring

My throat went dry as I stared into the Christmas package. That couldn't be . . . I couldn't be seeing what I *thought* I was seeing.

I swallowed hard, trying to work up some saliva. No go.

"Whaddya get?" Chet asked.

"Nothing," said Joe. He reached over my shoulder for the lid to the box. He was too slow. Brian whipped it out of his grasp.

"Are those . . ." Greg let his words trail off.

"They most certainly are," Brian answered, shooting me a you'll-never-live-this-down grin.

Mark began to giggle. Yes, giggle. Like a little girl.

"They have to be for somebody else," I stammered, feeling a blush rise from my neck up to my face. Usually it's only girls who get me blushing.

"No, no, no," Brian told me. "Don't worry." He waved the gift card in my face. "It says 'To Frank and Joe Hardy.' No one is going to try to take those Underoos away from you."

"Un-de-roos," Mark giggled out the word.

"Oooh, and they're Scooby Doo ones," said Chet. "He must be your favorite, because he's a detective too!"

Joe and I have a reputation around town for being amateur detectives. No one knows we're also members of ATAC, American Teens Against Crime, a secret organization that puts teens undercover to help bring down criminals.

I shoved the tissue paper back down over the— you knows. That's when I felt it. Something hard and thin under the—you knows. "We have to go put these away," I blurted out, jumping to my feet.

"Now? The game is starting," Greg protested.

"The game is starting!" Mark repeated. He instantly turned all his attention to the TV.

"Joe, come on," I urged.

"Frank has this thing about his underwear drawer," Joe explained. Not very helpfully. "He has a whole system. He's probably going to have to get out the label maker and everything."

to make fun of my label maker, but it useful lots of times. None of those times underwear drawer, though.

We'll be back in a minute," I said. Then I headed up the stairs, trying not to look like I was in too much of a hurry.

"We got an assignment?" Joe asked as he followed me into my room. "Or have you added even more freak to your neat freak-ness?"

I dug around in the box and pulled out a game cartridge. "We got an assignment," I answered. That's the way we always receive the details of our ATAC undercover missions—disguised as a game.

"Someone at ATAC is trying to develop a sense of humor," Joe commented. "And failing. I mean, Underoos. And Scooby Doo. They could have at least sent Spidey."

"The pizza delivery method of getting us the cartridges worked fine for me." I tossed the "game" to Joe. Airline tickets and some cash were also stashed at the bottom of the box.

"Where are the tickets to?" asked Joe.

I flipped open one of the folders. "Miami."

"Sweet sweetness," Joe said. Then he slid the game cartridge into my player.

A huge red-and-white-striped circus tent filled the screen. Yellow flags with black polka dots flapped in the breeze up top. The camera zoomed higher up. A blimp floated overhead. A sign in blinking lights on the side said FOOTBALL FRANKS SEMIFINAL HOT DOG EATING COMPETITION TODAY!

"It's that thing from the commercial we were just talking about," Joe said.

I nodded, without looking away from the monitor. The camera swooped down and entered the tent. A long, long table was set up in the center ring. I did a quick head count. Fifty teenagers sat there, mounds of hot dogs in front of them. Girls in spangled costumes twisted and twirled on ropes far over their heads.

"I don't exactly get how the thing with the girls and the ropes fits in with the eating," my brother commented. "But I like."

A drumroll started up. A spotlight snapped on. And a man in full ringmaster gear—red tailcoat and black top hat—stepped into it. "Welcome to the Football Franks Semifinals!" he cried.

The camera swept around to take in the cheering crowd. And the Football Franks hot dog vendors in every aisle.

"The winner of today's competition will go on to the finals, where they will have the chance to earn five hundred dollars for every inch of delicious Football Franks hot dogs they eat. That's six thousand five hundred dollars for each and every dog." He threw his gloved hands in the air, and the girls all gave an extra twirl on their ropes.

"The rules are very simple," the ringmaster continued. "The hot dogs may be eaten in pieces. Buns and meat may be eaten separately. Dipping food in water is allowed. Food in the mouth when the time is up does count, as long as it is ultimately swallowed. Finally, if there are any Roman incidents, the perpetrator will be disqualified."

"Roman incidents?" asked Joe.

"He has to be talking about puke. Romans weren't shy about vomiting during big meals. Some of them had one slave to wipe their mouths and another one under the table to clean up the mess," I explained.

"Gross," said Joe. "And how do you know this stuff?"

"It's in Seneca. The *Moral Epistles*," I told him.

"Of course it is," Joe muttered.

The sound of a shot jerked my attention back to the monitor. Just the starting pistol.

"Whoa." Joe shook his head in astonishment. "Look at them go. Do you see that girl on the end? She's so tiny. Her stomach has to be tiny. How is she fitting all that in?"

"Stomach size isn't related to—," I began.

"That guy's out," Joe said. "He's having a Roman incident all over the place."

The camera moved in on the vomiting guy. Then the image froze.

"This is David Cole," the voice of our ATAC contact announced. *"He died ten minutes after this video was recorded. An autopsy determined that the cause of death was poison."*

The image was replaced with a grinning David Cole wearing a crown. He had his arm around someone dressed as a giant hot dog.

"He looks . . ." Joe hesitated. "He looks just really happy."

"Yeah." It's always weird to see a picture of someone looking so happy and normal, goofy even, and know that they are dead.

"David had been participating in competitive eating contests for three years. He had won every contest he entered. He was considered the front-runner to win not only this semifinal contest, but the final to be held during halftime at the Super Bowl," our contact continued. *"We have determined that David was murdered. The most likely suspects are his competition. Your mission is to go undercover at the Football Franks Hot Dog Eating Contest and find David's killer."*

4.
Fully Loaded

"We need cool names. Competitive eater names," I told Frank as we started downstairs that night after everyone was asleep.

"Like that guy Cookie Monster," Frank said.

"Yeah. But more like the woman who calls herself the Praying Mantis. A praying mantis can eat a hummingbird. The female bites the male's head off after mating. That's an eater name that will make other people in a contest step back. I need a name like that." I walked into the kitchen and opened the fridge. Frank and I needed some practice materials.

"I don't think you're going to come up with a name that's actually going to scare the competitors," said Frank. "Especially since one of them is probably a killer," he added.

"We only have two packages of hot dogs. I guess we can start with them." I tossed the package on the counter. "We have a ton of carrots. We could cut them to the right length, but they're never going to be the right consistency. Or maybe we should begin with total baby steps. There's a bunch of Jell-O. That would be easy to swallow. The stuff we read on the Web said getting past the gag reflex is the big thing for gurgitators."

"We don't have much time to get all this stuff down, so—," Frank began.

"Duh. I know that much. We just spent the last three hours reading everything we could find on the Web on competitive eating," I interrupted.

Frank shook his head. "What I meant was, we don't have much time to prep for the mission to find the murderer." Have I mentioned that my brother has no sense of humor?

He got two packages of hot dog buns out of the cupboard. "I think we should start with the food we're actually going to be working with. We can baby-step it with the buns."

None of the big-time eaters ate the dogs and buns together in a competition. We'd already learned that much. "We need water for dipping," I reminded Frank as I laid the hot dogs on a plate for nukage.

"How long are we allowed to dip food in the contest?" Frank asked.

I could tell from the way he asked that he already knew the answer. Quizzing me is this annoying big-brother thing Frank does sometimes.

"Ummm, anywhere from an hour to thirty seconds, depending on if the bun is whole wheat or white, and in the case of the dog, if it is boiled, broiled, or barbecued." I stuck the plate of hot dogs in the microwave and got them going.

"Funny," Frank said.

As if he actually knows the definition of that word.

"Five seconds of dipping time max," I answered. I didn't want to give him an aneurysm or anything. He gets super serious right before a mission. Just because we're dealing with solving a murder. Jeez!

Frank poured two glasses of water and set them on the kitchen table. "We should go one at a time," he said. "Trying to eat this fast is dangerous. We should spot each other. You still remember how to do the Heimlich?"

"Yep."

"Okay, I'll go first." Frank grabbed a chair and ripped open a bag of buns. He dipped one in his glass of water, then shoved half of it in his mouth and swallowed it whole. "It's true what we read online. You really don't have to chew if you dip. Try it."

I folded a bun in half, dunked it for a count of three, then crammed the entire thing straight down my gullet. My gag reflex started up, but I willed the wet wad of bun to keep on going down. A big part of winning at competitive eating is mental, according to the major players.

I couldn't help giving a snort, and a little bit of bun came out of my nose. "That doesn't count as a Roman incident, right? Or what's that other thing they call it? A reversal of fortune?"

"I don't know what you'd call it, except truly disgusting," Frank said. "Just try not to do it again."

The microwave beeped, and I grabbed the plate of hot dogs and set them on the table. They smelled awesome. "I bet I could eat fifty-three and three-quarters of them, just like Ryuichi Shinseki in the Nathan's Famous contest in Coney Island," I bragged.

"Did you forget the part where Shinseki is supposed to have gastroptosis, that abnormal condition where the stomach can extend below the rib cage?" Frank asked.

"That's not why he won. You're doing him an injustice. It had nothing to do with having a freaky stomach. First, he has the right nickname.

Typhoon. A Typhoon is definitely going to crush a Praying Mantis or Cookie Monster! Second, he has the techniques. The Shinseki Shimmy and the Solomon method. We've got to get both of them down," I told him.

"We don't have to win the contest," Frank reminded me. "We just have to be convincing undercover."

"Convincing to a bunch of people who have each won a qualifying round," I countered.

Frank nodded. "Okay, so, the Solomon method." He picked up a hot dog and broke it in half. He put a half into each side of his mouth and pushed them in. Chomp. Chomp. Chomp. And the halves were down.

"How'd it feel?" I asked.

Frank took a swig of the water. "I know it's supposed to be like turning your throat into a two-track conveyor belt. But I think mine's only built wide enough for one." He took another long swallow of water. "I feel like there's a chunk of meat caught halfway down."

"Do you need me to Heimlich you?" I asked.

"You know the rule. If you can talk, you can breathe. And if you can breathe, you don't need the Heimlich," Frank said. "But I can see why the International Federation of Competitive Eating

28

discourages training at home. It would be way too easy to choke."

"You forgot to do the Shimmy," I reminded him. "Maybe that was the problem." I took a hot dog, broke it in half, and tried the double-track conveyor belt thing myself. Except as the meat was going down, I tried to wiggle my body the way I'd seen Shinseki do it in the YouTube clip Frank and I'd watched.

"Did it help?" Frank asked.

"Squirming around actually made me want to gag more," I admitted. "Let me try the chipmunk method." I grabbed a hot dog and bit it into small pieces as fast as I could. I used my tongue to shove the pieces over to the inside of my left cheek. I repeated with another hot dog until I could feel the skin on my left cheek bulging. Then I got the right cheek pocket filled with meat.

This was a good move for the last thirty seconds of the competition. If this was a contest, I'd get credit for all the hot dogs I had in my mouth when time was called—as long as I managed to swallow them. I didn't have to swallow them fast. I just had to get them down.

Frank watched me closely—to see if he needed to start a resuscitation—as I tilted my head back and tried to let some of the hot dog pieces slide down my gullet. I had the meat packed in so tight that at first it wouldn't budge. I had to waggle my jaws back and forth and twist my tongue around to jar some of it loose.

Then it was like a hot dog avalanche in my mouth. The pieces of meat tumbled out of my cheeks. My instinct was to jerk my head up and spit them out, but I just kept telling myself to relax. My throat muscles convulsed as the bits of hot dog moved down, but I managed to keep swallowing.

"You did it!" Frank cried.

I drained my glass of water. It was cloudy from the bun dunking, but it was the best thing I'd ever tasted.

"Yeah, I did it. I ate five whole hot dogs and a hot dog bun since we came down here. Big whoop." I shoved my hair off my forehead. It was damp with perspiration. "I think I'm already getting the meat sweats!"

Gurgitators got seriously sweaty when they gorged on meat. Something about the combo of protein and adrenalin.

"I think it's just the ordinary sweats," said Frank. "You haven't eaten enough protein to—"

"How's the prep going?" our dad asked from the doorway, interrupting Frank.

"Good," I answered.

"Great," Frank said, right on top of me.

We're the only two ATAC agents who actually live with one of the big bosses of the agency. *The* big boss, in fact. Our dad started ATAC. He's a retired cop. When he was on the force, he saw all the ways it would be useful to have teens undercover. Teens can fly under the radar. No one is expecting them to be working for the government. No one is expecting them to be thinking about anything but video games and popping their zits.

It's cool that Dad started ATAC. But what isn't cool is that he likes to keep a close eye on our missions. He's just trying to keep us safe. What he forgets is that we've had the same prep as every other agent. We're just as good at our job as every other kid out there.

Dad leaned against the doorjamb, trying to look all casual. "Competitive eating's a strange world, isn't it?" He shook his head. "The lengths some of the eaters will go to to stretch their stomachs. Eating cabbage and drinking gallons of water. All that water can—"

"Can poison you," Frank finished for him.

"Overdosing on water can mess up your electrolyte balance. Then you can end up getting a stroke or a heart attack. We learned that during our boarding-school hazing mission," I added.

I was trying to make two points to Dad. One, Frank and I aren't dumb—we know the dangers of the situations we get involved in. And two, we are experienced agents with a bunch of missions under our belts.

"Message received," Dad said, holding up both hands. "I know I don't have to worry about you guys. And I don't as ATAC agents. You both have excellent training."

Dad isn't dumb either.

He sighed. "I just can't help worrying about you as my sons."

Now what was I supposed to say? I never know what to say when Mom or Dad wants to get all heartfelt. I looked at Frank.

"We know, Dad," he said. "It's—"

"What's all this?"

Aunt Trudy had appeared behind Dad in the doorway. She was staring at the kitchen table as if it had burst into flames.

I followed her gaze to the remaining hot dogs and buns. "Just a snack, Aunt T," I told her.

"A snack?" she repeated. "We had a perfectly lovely dinner less than five hours ago. There was steak, and green beans, and baked potato, and rhubarb pie."

Suddenly it felt like a football game was going on in my gut. All that chow from dinner was going after a team made up of the dogs and buns. I pressed both hands over my belly, trying to calm things down in there.

Aunt Trudy clucked her tongue at me. "Look at Joe," she said to Frank and Dad. "He's trying to prove he's starving to death by clutching at his stomach like he's Oliver Twist. Well, it won't work."

She walked over to the fridge, pulled out a bowl of chili, and stuck it in the microwave. Then she took out relish, pickles, mustard, ketchup, sauerkraut, and grated cheese. She winked. "But if you're going to do it, do it right."

Two minutes later she had chili cheese dogs—fully, and I mean fully, loaded—for everyone. Everyone now included Mom, who had joined the group in the kitchen. "So what's the occasion for this late-night extravaganza?" she asked.

"I won tickets to the Super Bowl!" I exclaimed.

'Cause I am that good. I saw my chance to hand Mom and Aunt Trudy the perfect explanation for Frank's and my trip to Miami, and I took it. And the alibi would hold up even if they happened to see us in the crowd on TV.

"How?" Dad asked.

Just his little way of saying that if we wanted to be on our own, we were on our own.

No problem.

"Radio contest," I answered without hesitation.

"Yeah, he knew the name of Paris Hilton's little dog," said Frank. "He knows everything about Paris Hilton. He loves her."

I've told him he doesn't understand humor so many times. Why does he even attempt it?

"The Super Bowl. Wow. That sounds exciting," Mom said.

"Yeah. It comes with airline tickets and hotel and everything. The contest was for teens, so there will be chaperones," I told her, trying to get as many Mom-type objections out of the way up front. "I might have to be in some contest during halftime." I definitely wasn't mentioning competitive eating in front of Mom. If she saw that part on TV, we'd deal with it when we got home. "But the big thing is, it's the Super Bowl. You know how hard it is to get tickets to the Super Bowl?"

"I assume you're taking Frank," Aunt Trudy said.

"Unless you want to be my date, Aunt T." Just say it. I'm smooth.

Aunt Trudy laughed. "I guess this is an occasion that's worthy of my special chili cheese dogs." She held hers out in a toast. "To Joe and Frank going to the Super Bowl!"

We all clicked dogs. As I brought mine to my

mouth, the smell of the sauerkraut sent the Stomach Bowl into overtime. There was no way I could get even one bite of this monster dog down into my gut with all that going on.

In a few days you're going to be undercover as a competitive eater, I told myself. *Suck it up. Or maybe it should be, shove it down.*

It was one of the hardest things I've ever done as an ATAC agent. But I ate it. Every bite.

Then the nightmare happened.

Aunt Trudy handed me another chili cheese dog—fully loaded. Because "Joe can never stop at one."

"This place is . . . I don't actually possess the words to describe this place," I told Frank as we walked into the lobby of the Coconut Oasis Hotel.

"Don't tell Ms. Whitman that," Frank said.

Ms. Whitman is my English teacher. Frank just keeps on trying with the sense of humor thing, doesn't he?

There were so many windows in the lobby it might as well have been made of glass. I couldn't keep my eyes off the pool. I let Frank deal with checking us in as part of the Football Franks group while I stared.

For starters, it wasn't really just a pool. It was a

group of pools linked by rivers. The rivers clearly had currents, 'cause people were floating down them in inner tubes. No paddling required. There was one spot where you could stop your tube next to a little island bar and get yourself a soda before you went on your way. I needed to get me some of that action.

"Come on," said Frank. "I've got our key cards." He led the way over to the elevators—also glass.

"Did you see that pool? If the elevators weren't see-through, I'd change into my swimsuit on the way up. We don't have anything scheduled with the other eaters until dinner, right?" I asked.

The closest set of elevator doors opened with a soft *ping*. Frank and I got on. He hit the button for the seventeenth floor. "I want to go over our cover story one more time," he said. "And I want to review the info we have on the other contestants."

"We know all that stuff," I protested. "You and I are cousins. We're still using our regular names. We entered a hot dog eating contest for charity. It wasn't an official qualifying competition, but Mr. Poplin, the CEO of Football Franks, agreed to let us in the final because we raised so much money—at least according to the ATAC team leader posing as the head of a foundation."

ATAC had even gotten up support material on

us and the contest on the Net. They always came through with awesome backup.

The elevator stopped to pick up other passengers, so I had to zip it. Basic, very basic, ATAC training—never talk about a mission in earshot of anyone except another ATAC member.

The next stop turned out to be the seventeenth floor. There was a woman in the hall walking a cat on a leopard-patterned leash, so I had to continue to keep it zipped. But as soon as we stepped into the room and shut the door behind us, I started in again. There was no way I was missing out on that pool.

"We're undercover," I reminded Frank. "That means we're supposed to act normal. Normal kids staying at this place would be out in that pool. That's probably where all the other contestants are right this second. So let's go."

He didn't answer.

I turned to look at him. Frank's face was the color of a frog's belly. "What's wr—"

Then I saw them. The pictures all over the room. Taped to the walls, the closet, the mirror, the TV, the glass doors leading to the balcony.

Pictures of David Cole lying in his coffin. Each picture had a question scrawled beneath it in blood red marker:

Would you rather lose—or die?

5.
Lose—or Die?

My eyes darted from one photo to the next. David in his coffin. David in his coffin. David in his coffin. The room started to feel like it was spinning around me.

"Seems like ATAC called it right when they decided one of the competitors in the eating competition was the most likely murderer," Joe said.

I blinked a couple of times to clear my vision. Then I took down one of the pictures, touching only the edges. I didn't want to mess up the prints—if there were any. I read the words on the bottom aloud. "Do you want to lose—or die?"

I looked over at Joe. "Yeah. That definitely sounds like a warning from somebody who is willing to kill to win the contest."

"Make that kill again," Joe corrected.

"Good point," I agreed. "We figured the winner could walk away with almost four hundred thousand bucks in college money. I'd call that a motive."

"Well, now I'm really looking forward to dinner," said Joe.

"What?" I asked. How'd we get from talking about motive to talking about food?

"We're eating with all the contestants," he reminded me. "That means if we're right, we'll be eating with David Cole's murderer."

Joe and I were the first ones at the table in the hotel dining room reserved for the Football Franks Hot Dog Eating Contest competitors. We wanted as much time as possible to gather intel about our suspects.

I thought I spotted the first one approaching. A teen guy with hair so short it could barely be called hair was coming our way. "That's Jordan Watnabe, the winner of the contest in Springfield, right?" I whispered to Joe. We'd spent the last few hours reviewing all the facts we'd been able to find about the other eaters.

"His hair's even shorter than in the pic we saw, but yeah," Joe answered.

"This the Football Franks table?" Jordan asked. He rolled his eyes. "Dumb question, right?" He jerked his chin toward the big Football Franks sign in the middle of the table.

"This is the place," Joe told him. "We're Joe and Frank."

"I'm Jordan," he said.

"What do you think of the hotel?" I asked. I wanted to know if he'd gotten the special "welcome" Joe and I had. I figured the hotel question might get him to that topic.

"It's awesome," he said as he sat down next to me. "Did you guys know they have DVDs at the front desk you can check out? They have all the Super Bowls for the last ten years. I've been OD'ing on them," Jordan continued. "I still can't believe that day after tomorrow I am actually going to be at the Bowl, live and in person."

"Are you a Cowboys fan or a Patriots?" Joe asked.

"Are you kidding me? I'm from Chicago. The Bears are my boys. But if I have to choose between those other two, I guess I'd go with the Cowboys. Terrell is—"

A guy in a tie-dyed Buddha T-shirt stepped up to our table. "Frank Hardy, Joe Hardy, Jordan Watnabe." He pointed to each of us as he said our names.

Joe pointed back at him. "Kyle Skloot." Kyle was another one of the contestants we'd researched.

Kyle raised his eyebrows. "Ding! Ding! Ding! You are correct!" he said in a game show announcer voice. "Tell him what he's won." He grabbed the chair next to Jordan.

"So you've been studying up on the competition too, huh?" Kyle asked Joe. "Just so you know—I'm the one to worry about."

"You guys studied about each other?" Jordan's eyes widened. "Wow, hard-core."

"You want to win, you gotta know the weakness of your opponent," Kyle told him.

"Is that one of Buddha's sayings?" I asked, staring pointedly at Kyle's T-shirt.

Kyle ran his hand down the shirt. "I got this at a conference I went to on Zen meditation. It's just one of the techniques I've been using to train. I've studied *The Art of War*, too. And I've been following the exercise routine of one of Oprah's trainers." He glanced over at Joe again. "You keep on trying to find my weakness. You won't be able to, because it isn't there. For the past six months, when I haven't been in school or sleeping, I've been training for Sunday's competition."

"That is one intense dude," Jordan muttered.

I agreed. It made me wonder—was he intense enough to murder?

"Angie Bates! Douglas Carney!" Kyle called out, pulling me away from my thoughts. He did his pointing thing at two teenagers heading toward our table. The guy had red hair and

---

SUSPECT PROFILE

Name: Kyle Skloot

Hometown: Ojai, California

Physical description: Age 16, 5'7", approximately 155 lbs., light brown, curly hair, brown eyes.

Occupation: Student

Background: Only child; has competed and won in tennis, violin, chess, and badminton competitions.

Suspicious behavior: Has put his whole life on hold for the competition; ultracompetitive.

Suspected of: The murder of David Cole.

Possible motive: Determined to win the Football Franks Hot Dog Eating Contest.

---

almost more freckles than bare skin. The girl was tall with brown eyes and short brown hair. Not nearly Jordan short, but short. Short and puffy. With glasses.

"She won the contest in Texas. She chews gum almost constantly to build up her jaw muscles. Maybe because she's a girl, her muscles need that. He won the contest in Georgia. He's a one-food trainer," Kyle rattled off.

"Kyle has decided he's our emcee for the evening," Joe explained.

"Uh, hi," said Douglas.

Angie blew an enormous bubble as she sat down next to me. The smell of fruit mixed with mint hit my nose. "Kyle, huh?" she asked.

"Kyle Skloot," he answered. "Soon to be the winner of the Football Franks contest."

"But wait . . ." Angie furrowed her brow in fake concentration. "Aren't you the guy who wouldn't even be here if the other guy hadn't died?"

Joe shot me a look that was easy to understand—low blow. True. Not that Kyle didn't kind of deserve it for bragging his head off.

"I would have beaten David Cole," Kyle insisted.

Angie shrugged. "If you say so. It's just that he won the Hungry Boy Eat-off at the New York State

43

Fair last year. He won the pancake-eating contest they had when the one thousandth Pancake World opened—and that one had adults entered in it. He won the Pizza Pie—"

"We get it. He won some contests," Kyle interrupted. "But the thing is, I was never in one of those contests."

A super skinny blond boy rushed over and dropped into the last empty chair. "Sorry I'm late," he said.

Kyle pointed at him. "Vern Ricci." His voice wasn't as loud as it had been for his other name announcements. It seemed like Angie had gotten to him a little.

"Yeah, I'm Vern," the new guy said. He shoved his bangs out of his face. He had those emo bangs where the whole point of them seems for them to be *in* your face. Which seems kind of stupid to me. But, as Joe often points out, I don't have a very good understanding of current fashion trends.

A waitress arrived at the table less than ten seconds after Vern. "Looks like the whole group's here. Mr. Poplin from Football Franks asked me to tell you he's very sorry, but he isn't going to be able to join you for dinner. A conference call he was expecting hasn't come in yet and it will run late. He is in suite 1041 if you need him, and the entire hotel staff is available to assist you. He also said tomorrow's beach trip with him is on, and that you should all be sure to order whatever you like tonight. So what can I get you to start?" She looked over at Angie.

"I'd like six apples and thirty carrots—raw. And nine large salads," Angie answered.

The waitress didn't act surprised by the order. I figured she must have been prepped that this table would have some weird food requests.

"Clearly that's only what you eat when you get close to training," Kyle commented. "You don't get that body living off fruit and vegetables. Or that skin."

Angie was on the pudgy side, and her face was really broken out. But still. If Aunt Trudy was here, Kyle would be having himself a long time out right now.

Angie pulled down her glasses and stared at him for a long moment—then popped her gum in his direction and shoved her glasses back in place.

"And you?" the waitress asked Douglas.

"Twenty-two orders of buffalo chicken wings," he said, his voice low, his eyes on the table. "With mayonnaise. Lots of mayonnaise."

Kyle snorted. "Tell me you don't really believe

that mayonnaise lubricates your guts and makes it easier to get food down?"

Douglas shrugged. "It works for me."

Vern asked for water with lemon when it was his turn. "How many lemons?" the waitress asked.

"Just the usual," he told her. "A slice."

"Same for me," said Jordan. "I fast before competitions too. Got to free up the belly."

"Everybody knows fasting shrinks your stomach. A shrunken stomach plus a lot of food equals losing," Kyle said.

"It got both of us to the Super Bowl, didn't it?" Jordan asked.

"Yeah, and since you know everybody's stats, you probably know that Jordan got as many dogs into his belly at the Chicago regional as you did at the one in L.A.," Joe added.

Kyle flushed. "I'm not eating in front of you people," he announced, dropping the debate over the merits of fasting. "I spent months figuring out the perfect precompetition food regimen, and I don't plan on sharing it. I'll order from room service later," he told the waitress.

"Good. I think having to watch you eat would make me lose my appetite," Angie snapped. She seemed like a girl who had no problem standing up for herself.

The waitress looked over at Joe. He ordered every dessert on the menu, plus three sides of French fries. "I'm in the stomach-stretching camp. And if you can't have fun stretching your stomach before the contest, why even do it?" he asked.

Jordan was the only one who seemed to think that was funny. No one else cracked a smile. The contest was clearly way too serious for them to joke about.

The waitress turned to me. "I'll have two bowls of cooked cabbage and three bowls of oatmeal," I told her. "And can I have a pitcher of water?"

"Classic high-fiber, low-fat, high-water stomach-expanding technique," Kyle observed. "Classic, but way too safe to beat me."

"I think we may need to move you to a bigger table," the waitress told us. "There's not going to be room for all the plates, even with three of you not eating. I'll see what I can arrange." She hurried off.

"Maybe Kyle's ego could sit by itself," said Angie. She began unwrapping fresh sticks of gum—some watermelon, some peppermint. "That would clear up some space."

That got a laugh from everyone. Everyone but Kyle.

"Jordan, Joe, and I were talking about the hotel

before the rest of you got here," I said. I still wanted to find out if the others had gotten death threats.

"Yeah," Jordan jumped in. "Did you guys know you can get DVDs of the old Super Bowl games at the front desk? Right before dinner I was watching highlights from Super Bowl Eleven. Willie Brown made this awesome interception. I've gotta watch it again before I return it. It's a thing of beauty the way he got it before Fran Tarkenton and took it seventy-five yards for a TD. Seventy-five yards! Nobody broke that record for twenty-nine years!"

"We have the newest Xboxes in our rooms too. Did you see that?" I added quickly. I'd already figured out that Jordan was a guy who could talk about football a lot. Which would usually be great. But Super Bowl facts weren't going to help Joe and me solve the case.

"Yeah, that was a cool surprise," Joe said. "Although we got another surprise that wasn't so good. . . ."

I glanced around. Angie had lowered her glasses again to stare at Joe intently. Vern and Douglas suddenly looked especially interested.

"What kind of other surprise?" asked Angie.

"The artwork was kind of, uh, gross," I told her. "Usually hotels have pictures of flowers or boats on lakes, but our room was covered with—"

"Pictures of David Cole in his coffin!" Vern burst out.

Suddenly everyone at the table was talking.

"You too?" Angie exclaimed.

"I wasn't saying anything. I thought maybe they'd cancel the contest," said Kyle at the same time.

"I didn't want to say anything either. If my parents knew, they'd have me home yesterday," Jordan added. "And there was no way I was missing the Super Bowl."

"And anyway, it was just somebody's lame attempt at psychological intimidation," Kyle said. "Probably somebody at this table."

"Yeah, it's not like somebody offed David to get him out of the contest," said Angie. "He had some weird food reaction."

The fact that David had been murdered hadn't been made public yet. ATAC was keeping it quiet until Joe and I finished our investigation.

"I'm not going to let some jerk with a copier scare me away," Douglas said, speaking more loudly than he had all night.

Kyle knocked on the table until everyone got quiet. "So it's obvious we all want to keep this to ourselves, right?" He looked from person to person. "We don't want to risk the contest getting canceled, right?"

One by one, we all gave the same answer: "Right."

My heart started to thump against my ribs. Everyone at this table was in serious danger— except for the one person who was the killer.

Joe and I were going to have to keep a close watch at all times to make sure no one else ended up in a coffin like David Cole.

As all the contestants piled into one of those stretch SUVs for the beach trip the next morning, I did a quick evaluation of the group. No one looked like they'd spent the night sitting up in bed with the lights on, terrified that they might get killed. The pictures of David and the threats hadn't shaken them up too much.

I wasn't sure if that was good or bad. A little fear might help keep them safe.

A silver-haired man with a little mustache was the last one on board. "Hello, kids," he called out. "I'm Edward Poplin, owner and CEO of Football Franks."

Everybody let out a cheer in greeting, and Mr. Poplin smiled. "I apologize for not having dinner with you last night. I hope the hotel staff made sure you had everything you wanted and needed. You should feel free to call on them—or me—day or night." He turned his head toward the driver. "We're just waiting for one more, Wilson."

Wait. Had I missed somebody?

"We're all here," said Kyle.

"Douglas's sister is coming with us," Mr. Poplin explained. "She's around the same age as all of you. And besides, I'm renting surfboards for anyone who wants one. Candi's a professional surfer. I'm sure she'll be happy to give any of you tips if you need them, right, Doug?"

Douglas gave a weak smile. "Yeah, I guess," he mumbled.

"What do you mean, you guess?" a girl with sun-streaked brown hair asked as she climbed into the SUV-limo. "Of course I will. Sorry I'm late, you guys. I couldn't find my board wax for a minute."

Wilson, the driver, shut the door, and a moment later we were driving down one of Miami's palm-tree-lined streets.

"I have everyone's lunch order for the picnic. Now I just need a head count on the boards. Who's surfing?" Mr. Poplin asked.

He got a yes from everyone except Vern and Angie.

"I don't exercise before a competition," said Angie. "Walking down to the beach is more than I usually do. Mostly I exercise by thumb texting or clicking the TV remote."

"I try to sleep as much as possible when I'm prepping for a big eat. If I can't sleep, I try to stay very still," Vern explained.

"The Praying Mantis does two hours of aerobic exercise a day," Kyle told them. "It keeps her metabolism on fire."

Angie gave him what I'd decided was her fall-back response. She popped her gum in his direction. Vern just shrugged.

Our hotel was practically on top of the beach, so we'd barely gotten on the road before we stopped in front of Miami Phil's Surf Shop. Mr. Poplin led the way in and rented boards, wet suits, umbrellas, lounge chairs, and an inflatable sea horse. I wasn't sure who that was for. Maybe Mr. Poplin.

He also bought up one of every kind of sunscreen, some visors, and some floppy sun hats. "I don't want anyone getting heat stroke," he told us. "I want you all in top eating form for tomorrow."

"You don't have to worry about me. I live in top form," Kyle—who else—answered.

Joe elbowed me. "I've been discovered by the local talent," he said quietly. He jerked his chin toward two girls in bathing suits and flip-flops. They did seem to be checking Joe out.

"Here they come," he added under his breath. "You think Mr. Poplin would mind if I—"

The girls walked up to Joe—then passed him and kept right on walking. "You're Candi Carney, right?" the taller girl asked Douglas's sister.

Candi smiled like someone auditioning for a toothpaste commercial. "I sure am."

"Can I get your autograph?" The taller girl held out a copy of *Surf World* with Candi's picture on the front.

"Absolutely." Candi pulled a purple pen out of her pocket and signed the magazine cover with a flourish.

"Congratulations on winning the competition in L.A. last Friday," the other girl said. "We watched you on ESPN. You were outrageous on that last wave."

"My parents are always joking that they're going to have to buy a bigger house so they'll have a place to keep all my trophies." Candi laughed. The girls did too. I noticed that Douglas didn't.

"They might have one of mine after this weekend," he said.

"That's my brother, Dougie," Candi explained to the girls. "He's going to enter a contest tomorrow to see who can eat the most hot dogs. You should see how hard he's been training."

That did get a little smile out of Doug, until his sister added, "Every Tuesday night, no matter what, Dougie would trudge down to the all-you-can-eat buffet at Clucky's Chicken House and eat until he almost puked. It's been so, so hard for him."

That got the girls and Candi laughing again. And in an at-Doug way. Not in a with-Doug way.

"Okay, troops, we're heading out," Mr. Poplin called from his spot in front of the cash register. "Everybody grab something and take it out to the SUV. We'll have you in the water in ten minutes, tops."

Mr. Poplin's prediction was accurate. In nine minutes, everybody was in the warm Miami Beach ocean, except Angie and Vern. I could see them on the beach as I straddled my board in the lineup. That's the spot just outside where the waves are breaking. Surfers wait there for their rides.

Angie had to be broiling sitting out in the sun in her sweat suit. But she claimed that sweating, without burning calories by exercising, was part of her regimen. Vern was stretched out in a beach chair with a massive jug of aloe vera juice at his side. The only thing he wanted to do was doze and get the juice down before lunch.

I turned my head, checking out the waves that would be coming in. A flash of something gray not too far from Joe caught my eye. A dolphin? We'd heard that sometimes they came up to swimmers. Getting some up-close-and-personal time with a dolphin would be pretty cool.

I squinted, raising my hand to block some of the sun. There. I saw the flash of gray again. A fin. But not the right size or shape.

The skin on the back of my neck began to crawl. That wasn't a dolphin.

"Joe!" I shouted as loudly as I could. "Behind you! Shark!"

6.

Black Eyes of a Great White

Flat on my belly on the board, I paddled for shore as hard as I could. A beautiful monster wave was rising up underneath me. I felt the back of the board lift. Oh, yeah!

"Shark!" I heard Frank yell. "Behind you!"

Automatically, my body continued through the surfing motions. I pushed up and popped to my feet. Then I managed a glance over my shoulder as I started to ride down the wave's face.

The first thing I saw was Jordan, starting his own ride. Then I saw it. The three-foot dorsal fin. Moving in on Jordan.

To the shark, I knew Jordan—in his dark wet suit—had to look like a nice, juicy seal. I had to get to him. Fast.

Before my patch of wave flattened out too much, I started my turn. I leaned back a little but kept my board flat. I didn't want to lose any speed.

Do it! Now! I told myself. I pressed down on my heels, lifted the balls of my feet. My board reversed directions. I brought my body around with it.

Then I did the thing they teach you never to do, starting with your first surfing lesson. I aimed myself at Jordan. I struggled to keep on my feet as the wave's force hit me.

My board hit Jordan's with a sickening crunch. And then we were both in the water. I yanked off the leash connecting me to my board. Yanked off Jordan's, too.

Now where was the shark? I couldn't have knocked Jordan very far out of its path. And it had been powering straight at him.

The sea salt burned my eyes as I stared through the water. A shadow flicked past me on the right. I whipped toward it. And I saw the great white's blank black eyes on me.

They began to roll back. Showing some white. I knew that's what happened right before a shark struck. *Gills*, I told myself. *Go for the gills*. I curled my hands into claws and kicked hard, moving in.

An arrow of green lasered through the water. It

ran across the shark. Found one of its eyes. And stayed there.

With its tail thrashing, the shark retreated. I goggled, hardly able to believe what had just happened.

What are you doing? I screamed at myself. *Get out of here!*

I whipped around and I followed the laser to its source. Frank. Holding the latest ATAC underwater gadget. We'd never had the chance to try it out before.

He pointed toward shore. Jordan didn't need more than that. He started swimming. Frank and I were right behind him.

I had to sit down as soon as I made it out onto the beach. It was like my entire body had gone the consistency of a jellyfish.

A few people were still scrambling out of the ocean. Lifeguards had put out the alarm. They were getting everybody back on the shore.

"Everybody from our group in?" Mr. Poplin called.

"Yeah," Angie answered. She turned to Frank. "Vern and I heard you scream, and we got the lifeguards. They were on it so fast."

"Good." Frank dropped down next to me.

Jordan stayed on his feet, staring out into

the water. "Where is it? Where'd it go?"

I shook my head. "I don't know. Maybe it's already heading back out to deep water." I didn't see its fin anywhere.

"What was that thing you used on it?" Jordan asked Frank.

Frank pulled out the laser. It didn't look like anything more special than a large waterproof pen. "It's a laser pointer that scuba instructors use to show things to their students. Green is the color that shows up best underwater. I just shined it in the shark's eyes. Their eyes are really sensitive."

It was a little more than that, but the explanation seemed to work for Jordan.

"Yeah, I heard that about their eyes," I added. "I read that they roll them back in their heads when they're going to attack, to protect them." That's how I'd known the great white was this close to taking a bite out of me before Frank swam to the rescue.

"Lucky you had that thing," said Douglas, joining us near the edge of the water. Candi and Vern came with him.

"Really lucky. I ordered it online and I thought maybe I'd have a chance to try it out during the trip. Maybe in the hotel pool!" Frank answered.

"I think the pool is where we should all be right now," Mr. Poplin said. "What about the rest of you? Should we move this party poolside?" His voice was cheery, but his face was still pale.

"I don't know if I want to be in a pool right now. Would it be okay if I went to my room and watched some more Super Bowl DVDs?" asked Jordan.

"Whatever you want," Mr. Poplin said. "Kyle, we're going to get packed up," he called. Kyle stood about twenty feet down the beach. He didn't turn toward Mr. Poplin or give any indication that he'd heard.

"Kyle!" Mr. Poplin called again.

Kyle slowly bent and picked up something at his feet. Then he turned toward us and held it up. It was Jordan's surfboard. And it had been bitten in half.

I couldn't take my eyes off the board as Kyle walked over to us. All I could think about was those same jagged tears in Jordan's body. There's no way he would have survived.

Kyle silently handed the board to Jordan. I think it was the first time since Frank and I met him that Kyle had done anything silently. Something metallic on the board caught the sun, and the glare blinded me for a second.

"What's that?" asked Angie. She reached out

and fingered the metallic object on Jordan's surf-board. "It's vibrating."

"That's weird. I've never seen anything like that on a board before. Does anyone else have one?" Frank asked. He got no's and head shakes from the group.

"It's not anything I've ever seen," Candi added. "And I've seen everything anybody's put on a board."

Frank leaned close to the metallic device. "Angie's right. It's definitely putting out vibrations."

"Maybe that's why the shark went right for Jordan," said Candi. "One of my surf instructors told me that sometimes motorboats running at slow speeds get attacked by sharks. That's because the motor is giving out vibrations that are like the ones wounded animals make. The sharks think something is dying and come to check it out."

Mr. Poplin took the board out of Jordan's hands. "I'm taking this to the surf shop right now. I want to know exactly what this device is and why it was on this board. I'll send Wilson back to help you get everything loaded up."

"Can I go with you?" Candi asked. "I want to hear what they say."

"If you'd like." He strode off toward the wooden

steps that led to the parking lot. Candi trotted behind him.

"There's no way the surf shop had anything to do with that thing being on the board," Kyle said. He'd found his voice again.

"Kyle's right. Somebody knew the vibrations would attract a shark," Vern put in, shoving his long bangs out of his face. "Somebody wanted it to happen."

"You're saying somebody wanted to kill me?" Jordan burst out.

"Don't act so surprised. Did you forget those death threats we all got in our rooms?" Vern asked.

"We all decided those were just scare tactics," Jordan protested. He paced around in a tight circle. I could practically see all the excess adrenaline in his body looking for a place to go.

"Maybe we were stupid," said Angie. She blew a big bubble, so big it almost touched the lenses of her glasses.

"So then that means somebody killed David Cole!" Vern cried, his voice about twice as high as usual. "Who's going to get killed next?"

"Easy, guy," I said. "We all have to stay calm."

"Why?" Vern demanded. "Am I supposed to just stay calm so one of you can kill me?"

"Wait. One of us?" asked Douglas, folding his arms across his chest.

"Of course one of us," Vern shot back. "Who else but one of us cares enough about the competition to kill somebody?"

"Makes sense to me," Kyle said. "And you know who I think the most likely killer is? Somebody who didn't go into the water. If I tried to sic a shark on somebody, I'd definitely keep my behind on the beach."

Vern threw up his hands. "So you're saying I did it?"

"You stayed out of the water. That's what I'm saying," Kyle told him.

Good point.

"Kyle, you were sitting right next to David at the L.A. contest," Douglas said softly, eyes on his feet.

"What?" Kyle exploded.

"You were sitting next to him. You could have done something to his food if you wanted to," Douglas mumbled.

"Wait, you were in L.A. too!" Kyle accused. "Those girls in the surf shop were talking about your sister being in a surfing competition there last Friday. There's no way you were in L.A. the weekend of the eating contest without going. That's how you know where I was sitting!"

SUSPECT PROFILE

<u>Name</u>: Vern Ricci

<u>Hometown</u>: Madison, Wisconsin

<u>Physical description</u>: 5'11", 119 lbs., blond hair, green eyes.

<u>Occupation</u>: Student

<u>Background</u>: Regular contributor to the Op-Ed page of the local paper; writes Meek One blog.

<u>Suspicious behavior</u>: Chose not to go swimming when Jordon was attacked by the shark; had access to Jordan's board.

<u>Suspected of:</u> The murder of David Cole; the attempted murder of Jordan Watnabe.

<u>Possible motives</u>: To eliminate competition and win the Football Franks Hot Dog Eating Contest.

"I didn't do anything," Douglas protested. "I just watched."

Was that true? I wasn't sure. Douglas being at the competition when David died made him a strong suspect.

"You both were in the SUV with Jordan's surfboard. Who knows—one of you might have even carried it out of the shop," Angie pointed out. "Either of you could have put that vibrating thing on it."

"You were in there too," Kyle said. "All of us were. And we all carried stuff out to the SUV."

True. And all of them had a motive for murder.

7.

Flying Hardy Brothers

"So we can eliminate Jordan as a suspect," I said. Joe and I were sitting on the balcony of our hotel room. We'd decided to skip the pool and spend the time going over the case.

And, okay, neither of us was all that excited about getting in the water again. Even highly chlo-rinated, fairly shallow, no-way-a-shark-could-be-in-here water.

"Yeah. Maybe a killer would stage an attack on himself so he would look less guilty. You know, 'Hey, I'm not the murderer, because somebody tried to murder me,'" Joe said. "But nobody would stage an attack involving a great white. It's not like you can hand one a hundred and say, 'Make it look real, but no teeth marks.'"

"Jordan never seemed to have quite as strong a motive as everyone else, anyway," I commented.

Joe took a long swig of his soda and propped his feet on the balcony railing. "You mean because he seems a lot more interested in the Super Bowl than in the eating competition?"

"Yeah. It's like he wanted to win the qualifying competition so he could come to the game. He didn't need David dead for that—they were in separate regional contests."

"And Jordan's here now. He's going to see the game no matter what. He's got what he wants. He probably wants to win the competition, too—who doesn't want to win? I want to win myself!" Joe said. "But he doesn't seem like somebody who wants to win bad enough to kill for it."

I tilted my head back and let the sun beam down on my face as I thought. "Everyone in the competition could have gotten to this level whether or not David died except—"

"Except Kyle," Joe finished for me.

"Right," I said. "He might have beaten David. But David had won a lot of other competitions."

"David had a good chance of mopping the floor with Kyle," Joe added. "No matter how much Kyle talks about how he's the best gurgitator ever born."

"And Kyle was sitting right next to David during the competition. Easy access to his food," I reminded Joe.

"Kyle could definitely win a Top Suspect contest." Joe drained his soda and picked up another can. His fourth.

"Aunt Trudy wouldn't approve," I said.

"Do you see Aunt Trudy around?" Joe shaded his eyes and stared in all directions. "Besides, I'm stretching my stomach for tomorrow." He popped the top of the can. "Douglas is a good runner-up for the Top Suspect prize. He was at the contest where David died too. Not quite as close, but there."

I took my laptop off the little table next to my lounge chair and flipped the lid up. "I wonder if anyone else from the group was in the vicinity when David died."

Joe moved his chair closer to my lounger so he could look over my shoulder. I went to YouTube and quickly found a bunch of clips of the L.A. contest. I love YouTube. There's almost nothing somebody hasn't posted a clip of.

I clicked on the first one. And we were back inside that red-and-white-striped tent. "You watch the left side of the crowd. I'll watch the right," I told my brother.

I started at the top row of spectators I could see and methodically moved my eyes from left to right, taking in each little face. I'd definitely need to play the clip again, but it was better to go slow and be thorough. Especially because the killer might have worn some kind of disguise. Would have if they were smart. And I gotta say, that vibrator device on the surfboard—very smart.

"Oh, man!" Joe exclaimed.

"What? Did you see someone?"

"Oh, yeah. Look at her." Joe tapped the screen. "Wow. Now I'm starting to understand that song Dad sings in the shower. 'I wish they all could be California girls.'"

In age, my brother isn't that much younger than I am. In maturity level—we're hardly even the same species.

 JOE

Joe here. I'm not letting that go by. My brother's problem is that girls scare him. They scare him because they make him stammer and blush and look like an idiot in pretty much any way possible.

Out. This is my part of the story.

"Joe, let me remind you of a couple of things. The eating contest is tomorrow. Somebody is trying to eliminate the competition. That means that somebody else could die—before tomorrow—if we don't stop them," I said, slowly and carefully. "So do you think you could look for our suspects instead of cute girls?"

"So you admit it—you think she's cute?" asked Joe.

"Joe, the people in the crowd are so small, I don't know how you could see enough to get one of your crushes." I restarted the clip from the beginning.

"I saw long blond hair," Joe said. "And she had her legs stretched out on the seat in front of her. The hair and those legs had to belong to a cute girl."

"You're quite the detective," I muttered as I continued my examination of my half of the crowd.

We didn't spot Vern, Angie, or Jordan in any of the clips—and with all the clips combined, there were shots of everyone in the tent. We did see Douglas near the front of the crowd, almost directly behind David. But we didn't catch him doing anything suspicious. It looked like he was taking notes. We didn't spot Kyle doing anything suspicious either.

Also, for the record, Joe "almost completely confirmed" that the spot on his California girl's stomach revealed by her low-rise jeans was "an adorable little tattoo."

"Okay, so as far as we know, only Douglas and Kyle were at the scene of David's murder and Jordan's attempted murder," Joe said. "Whaddaya say we tie them up and beat a confession out of them?"

I ignored him. Sometimes that's all you can do with Joe.

"Okay, okay. So, whaddaya say we find a way to get them out of their rooms and search for evidence?" he asked.

I laughed. "Great idea." I powered down the laptop. "So how do we get them out?"

"Maybe we could tell them Mr. Poplin wants to meet with them," Joe suggested.

He was on a roll. "There are a bunch of little conference rooms on the second floor. Let's give the guys notes telling them to meet him in one of them." I stood up and headed inside. I got a couple of sheets of hotel stationery from the little desk in the corner. "Mr. Poplin doesn't seem too formal, does he?" I asked.

"Formal? Have you forgotten those shorts he had on today? They could have put out somebody's eye, they were so bright," Joe answered.

"True." I grabbed a pen and sat down. *Hi, Douglas*, I wrote. *We need to have a quick chat. Meet me in the*— I looked over at Joe. "What's the name of one of those rooms?"

He flipped through the leather folder with all the hotel info in it. "Manatee," he told me.

Manatee Room, I wrote. *Second floor. 4:30. See you then. Edward P.* I wrote an identical note for Kyle. Well, identical except for the "Hi, Douglas" part. Then Joe and I took them down to the lobby and gave them to the woman working the front desk.

"How do we get in?" Joe asked as we crossed the lobby back to the glass elevators. "We'll be too exposed trying to pick the locks in the hallway. There are always people around."

"I have a plan," I told him.

"We had to be on the seventeenth floor," Joe muttered as he used one hand to swing out from our balcony and his other hand to catch the railing of the next balcony over.

"It's not like you'd break fewer bones if you fell

72

from the thirteenth floor," I told him.

"Hotels don't have thirteenth floors," Joe said as I started my swing. "Too many people don't want to stay on them. So they skip from twelve to fourteen. Is fourteen still unlucky then? 'Cause it's still the thirteenth even though it's not called that."

I hoisted myself over the balcony railing and landed in a crouch. "I don't think thirteen is unlucky anyway."

We monkeyed our way over two more balconies. Lucky for us it was February, so it was already starting to get dark. Otherwise a lot more people would be sitting outside. "This is it. Kyle's room," said Joe. Fortunately for us, all the balconies in sight were empty.

I pulled out my lock pick and got to work on the sliding glass door. It was no problem. ATAC had trained us on all kinds of locks. "We need to get this done fast. Who knows how long Kyle will wait for Mr. Poplin?"

"Since it's Mr. P., he'll probably wait for a while," Joe said, already moving toward the dresser. I headed to the closet. Nothing in there but clothes. I felt the pockets. Nothing.

"He has this log book of his training," Joe said, as I began searching under one of the beds. "It's intense. He's scheduled every minute of every day—down to two minutes for brushing his teeth after each meal. If this is accurate, the guy hasn't watched *The Simpsons*, or gone online, or played b-ball or anything that's just for fun in months. That'd make most people crack."

"Yeah." I hadn't found anything under the beds or under the mattresses or in the pillowcases. I started on the nightstand. Just books. *The Art of War. In It to Win It. Meditation for Dummies.*

"I found a major stash of bran and bottled water, but nothing like evidence yet," Joe announced. He got up on a chair and started feeling inside the light fixtures. I felt the hems of the curtains to see if anything had been slid inside. Checked the toilet tank. Checked the trash.

Joe checked for any loose carpet. Ran his hands over the backs of the furniture. Opened the mini-fridge. Took some macadamia nuts. Mr. Poplin had said we could eat anything in them, so . . .

"So we got nothing," he said, chomping on the nuts. "Just verification that Kyle takes the competition incredibly seriously."

"Let's get to Douglas's room," I answered. We walked back out to the balcony. I slid the door shut behind us and relocked it.

Getting to Douglas's room was going to be a little trickier. It was on the sixteenth floor. I leaned out over the railing of Kyle's balcony as far as I could. "I don't think anyone's out on the one below us," I told Joe softly.

"Here goes nothing," he said. He grabbed the top of the railing with both hands, then swung his legs over to the outside. He couldn't drop straight down. Otherwise he'd—drop straight down. All the way to the ground.

So he swung his body out and back, like he was doing a move on the parallel bars. Out and back. Out and back. Getting momentum. Out and—he let go. Angling his body in toward the balcony. When I heard him land with a thump, I let out a breath I hadn't even realized I'd been holding.

My turn. I rubbed my hands on the front of my khakis to make sure they were absolutely dry, then I grabbed the railing and launched my legs over. The weight of my body pulled on the tendons of my arms.

Don't just hang there, I ordered myself. *Get moving.*

I imitated Joe, swinging my legs back and out, then in again. Trying to get higher with each repetition. On the third swing I was high enough to see the balcony below me. I pointed my toes toward it. And I let go of the railing. A second later Joe was hauling me to my feet.

"I was thinking if we get tired of ATAC, we could

join the circus. The Flying Hardy Brothers," he said.

"Douglas's room is one to the left," I told him. The climb between balconies on the same floor seemed a lot easier this time. And we didn't even have to pick Douglas's door. He'd left it unlocked. "Guess he didn't think anybody would be crazy enough to climb in way up here."

"He doesn't know the Flying Hardy Brothers," Joe said, leading the way inside.

Douglas's room was a lot messier than Kyle's, which made it a little harder to search. For starters, his clothes were scattered all over the floor, not hung in the closet, so that made my pocket search slower. I had to make sure to leave everything positioned exactly as it had been, even though I thought it was really unlikely Douglas would notice.

"Ew," said Joe.

I jerked myself up from the floor, where I'd just begun my under-the-bed investigation. "What?"

"Douglas has his mini-fridge filled with mayo. I'm talking filled. There's nothing else in there," Joe told me, his face screwed up in an expression of disgust.

"I guess that explains that." I pointed to the large spoon covered with crusty white gunk sitting on his nightstand.

"Oh, man, he eats it straight? I'm going to go search the bathroom, since I may have to puke." Joe hurried off.

I got back on my stomach to check under the bed. I found another mayo-crusted spoon. But I scored big when I looked under the mattress. "Our boy keeps a journal," I called to Joe.

"Excellent. Read me the highlights," he said, reappearing from the bathroom. "Nothing in there, by the way." He moved on to searching for any loose patches of carpet or baseboard.

I opened the journal. It never feels right to look at something so private. But the information in here could save someone's life. "The first entry is about his sister," I said. Then I started to read. "'I wonder what would happen to Candi if she ever lost at anything. I think it might be like popping a hole in a helium balloon. I think she'd just shrivel up until she was this piece of trash.'"

Joe snorted. "Nice."

"Here's another one. 'Candi brought home another trophy. Does she even get that that's why Mom and Dad pay so much attention to her? Or does she think that it's actually about *her*? Like the actual her? If she stopped winning, she'd see. They'd treat her like they do me.'"

"Douglas acts like he's practically invisible," Joe commented. "He talks so quietly. And he's almost always looking down. Maybe it's because he feels . . . it sounds like he feels worthless."

"It also sounds like the only way he thinks he'd be worth anything is if he handed his parents a trophy," I added. "That's a pretty strong motive." I continued to flip through the journal, skimming. "There's some stuff about school. About how his homeroom teacher hasn't even figured out his name and the year's half over. Lots more Candi and parents stuff. A little bit about his dog. He seems to like his dog, at least, and seems to think his dog likes him."

I slid the journal back under the mattress. "Well, we don't have to do any more balcony climbing. We can just check the hall through the peephole and go out the front door when it's clear."

"I'm almost done. I only have to check the back of the dresser." Joe pulled it away from the wall and ran his fingers over it. "Clean," he announced. "Let's—"

We both froze as we heard the click of the key-card being swiped. Joe shoved the dresser back into place, and we bolted. At least we didn't have to worry about relocking the door.

Douglas's curtains were partially shut, and they

blocked us as we swung our way over to the next balcony.

We were safe.

Until Joe backed up a step and bumped into a large ceramic planter with a little palm tree in it. It teetered. I grabbed for it, but it went down. And it shattered.

The noise was horrible.

The next sound was worse. A voice from the shadows.

"I guess I need to call security."

8.
Caught!

We were caught!

I took a step forward. Then I smiled. I couldn't help it. Yeah, we were caught. But we were caught by a girl. Even in the dark I could see she was super cute in her cutoff shorts and bikini top. With her long blond hair falling almost to her waist. If you're going to get caught, that's the way to get caught. Am I right?

Frank didn't seem to think so. He looked like he was considering jumping. That's the way he gets around girls, especially girls of the super cute variety.

"Shouldn't I be calling security? Is there a reason not to?" the girl asked in this Southern accent that somehow multiplied the cuteness factor. Her words were sort of a threat. But the way she was looking at Frank wasn't. Obviously, she liked what she saw.

I kicked Frank in the shin, then gave him a big smile. I was hoping he would take the hint and smile at the girl. Maybe do a little flirting. I would be happy to do it. But she wasn't looking at me the way she was looking at Frank.

Frank blinked a few times. Then he seemed to process the situation correctly. It's a good thing it was dark, because I knew he had to be blushing. "Um, hi. Uh, no. There's no . . . you don't need to call security. We're harmless." He smiled at her.

I could almost see her getting melty around the edges. It was kind of sickening.

"Harmless, huh?" S.C., as in Super Cute, asked. She took a step closer, and a band of light from her room angled across her stomach. She had the cutest little bumblebee tat next to her belly button. And with her closer, I could smell something minty and fruity. I didn't know if it was a mix of shampoo and perfume or what, but I liked it. "What is a harmless guy doing sneaking around a balcony that isn't his?"

She didn't even say *guys*. Hello? Had I gone invisible?

"Good question," said Frank. At least he'd

stopped um-ing and uh-ing. "My brother and I were trying to see if we could make it all the way down the row of balconies without—"

"Breaking your necks?" S.C. interrupted.

"Yeah." Frank smiled again. "It's a guy kind of thing."

"So I couldn't understand?" asked S.C. The accent was killing me. It sounded like cotton candy tastes. Ms. Whitman, my English teacher, would be proud of that metaphor.

FRANK

Frank here. She'd be proud if you realized that it's a simile.

JOE

Out. My section.

Anyway, Frank managed to answer S.C., even though he is an idiot around girls. "Probably not," he said. "We didn't mean to scare you or anything. We were just going to go right by. But my brother accidentally took out your plant."

S.C. glanced over at it. "I think it'll live. I hope

you do. Go ahead with your balcony thing." She waved as Frank and I trotted in front of her and swung off her railing.

When we got to the balcony under ours, I stood up on the railing. With my arms stretched over my head, I could just grab the edge of our balcony floor with my fingers. I hoped aerobic exercise really was the way to prep for an eating competition, because I was definitely getting me some as I pulled myself up until I could brace my toes on the balcony too. Then I climbed over.

"Home at last!" I exclaimed as I collapsed on the nearest lounge chair. I stared at Frank as he made his landing. "I just don't get what's so special about you," I said.

"What?" Frank grabbed a half-empty soda and took a long drink.

"I mean, why do girls always stare at you when I'm standing right there?" I complained. "Maybe it's because I'm so good-looking I intimidate them. Yeah, I can see that. I'm all blond and everything. And everyone knows girls prefer blondes. They probably feel more comfortable with you, because they don't think somebody like you—a more ordinary guy—will reject them."

"Is it possible for you to stop thinking about girls until we find the killer who is on the loose?"

Frank asked. "I could hardly get you to focus on looking for our suspects in those video clips."

I leaped to my feet as if I'd been electrocuted and rushed inside. I powered up the laptop.

"Are you working?" Frank asked me from the doorway. "I can't believe it. I don't think you've ever in your life actually listened to me. At least not so fast."

I got to YouTube, found one of the clips we'd watched earlier, and clicked it. Where was she? Where was she?

There!

I hit pause. "Look at that girl!" I ordered Frank.

"What did I just say about the girl thing?" he asked.

"Look at her!" I tapped the screen.

"We discussed her before—her long hair, and her long legs, and the almost certainty of . . . a tattoo on the stomach." There it was. The lightbulb slowly flickering to life over his head.

"It's her, right?" I asked. "I know it was dark, but it's gotta be her. Long blond hair. The legs. The dark spot on her stomach I thought was a tat and the bumblebee tattoo are in exactly the same place."

"I think we have a new suspect," Frank told me. "You rock!"

"Let's go talk to her." I stood up and we hurried out of the room. We took the stairs down to the sixteenth floor. Neither of us wanted to bother waiting for the elevator.

"It should be room 1609," Frank said as we walked down the hall. "Her balcony was right next to Douglas's."

"This is it, then." I knocked on the door. No one answered, but I heard soft shuffling sounds inside. I knocked again.

"Keep your pants on," a familiar voice called. A familiar voice that so didn't remind me of sweet cotton candy. "I'm coming."

More shuffling. Then the door swung open. Angie stood there, her hair wrapped in a towel. Her face looked even blotchier than usual. "Sorry. I was in the shower. Obviously." She swept her hand down, indicating her floor-length robe. "What's up? Did the time change for dinner?"

"Hey, Angie. Actually, we wanted to talk to, I guess it would be your roommate," I said.

"What roommate?" she asked.

Frank and I exchanged a confused glance. "We met a girl earlier today," I explained. "Blond. About as tall as you. Kinda thin. Southern accent. Frank immediately got a big crush on her. He thought she told him this was her room."

"Well, she must have wanted to ditch him, because I'm the only one in here," said Angie.

I slapped Frank on the shoulder. "Frank, dude, that's cruel and unusual." I looked back over at Angie. "Have you seen a blond girl like that anywhere around? Maybe Frank just heard her wrong and she lives in one of the rooms right near you."

"I don't really stalk my neighbors," Angie said. "And I don't think it's a good idea for you—"

Before she could finish, a scream cut through the hallway. Long, and loud, and terrified.

9.

Strike Position

"It's coming from down there!" I yelled. I took off down the hall, Joe and Angie right behind me.

The scream came again. The sound made the hair on my arms stand up.

"I think that's Vern!" Angie exclaimed. "That's his room right there! With the door partway open."

"Slow down. Don't just run in," I ordered. "We don't know what's in there." The door was ajar. I pushed it a little wider. I heard Angie suck in her breath as she saw what was inside.

Vern sat motionless on the bed. A rattlesnake lay less than two feet away from him.

Cautiously I moved into the room, looking for a weapon. I grabbed the only thing I saw that might work—the lamp off the dresser.

87

The snake gave a rattle of warning at the motion. It curled the bottom half of its body into a defensive coil and raised the rest of its body into the air.

"Don't," Vern said, his voice tight. "If you get close enough to hit it, it could bite you." He gave a laugh that was on the edge of crying. "Or me."

"He's right, Frank. They're supposed to be able to strike as far as half their body length," Joe agreed. "I'll go find something we can use." He disappeared out the door.

"Okay, let's all just stay very still," I said. "It's probably more scared of us than we are of it. Let's not give it any reason to freak out."

Vern gave a fractional nod.

I kept my eyes on the snake. It seemed like every nerve in the rattler's body was focused on Vern.

I flexed my fingers on the base of the lamp. How long should I wait without taking any action? I'd told Vern and Angie that we shouldn't give the snake a reason to freak out. The thing was, it already looked freaked. It was holding its body in strike position. It was giving warning rattles.

When it moved to strike, it would be too late to do anything. It would happen way too fast for us to even see it. Forget about stop it.

I heard footsteps in the hall, then Joe crept back into the room, Douglas with him. Joe held a large garbage can. Slowly, he raised it in the air, then glanced over at me. I nodded. I thought it might work. It was our best chance.

In one fast movement, Joe stepped forward and brought the can down over the snake. I heard it strike the plastic. Its fangs would have gone into Joe's calf if the garbage can hadn't been between them.

Vern scrambled off the bed and backed up until he hit the sliding door across the room. Joe stayed where he was, with both hands firmly on the top of the can. We could hear the snake whipping around underneath it, tail rattling.

"I'll call the front desk," Angie said. She inched around Joe, heading for the phone. The can jerked, and she pressed her hands over his, her head tight against his arm.

"I'm okay," Joe told her. "Go phone." Angie slowly released her hands and continued to the nightstand.

"How did it get all the way up here?" Vern asked. "It's the sixteenth floor."

"It would have needed help," muttered Douglas.

"Help like the shark had help attacking Jordan," Joe suggested.

I tried to take in everyone's reaction at once. Everyone was looking down at the garbage can. Everyone looked scared.

Angie rejoined the group. "They're sending somebody up right now," she said. "I think Mr. P. should get some serious bucks taken off his bill."

"It's not the hotel's fault if somebody brought the snake in," Vern said.

"I didn't even think of that. I can't believe I didn't think of that. After Jordan almost got chomped on. And David . . ." Angie let her words trail off. She chewed hard on her watermelon and peppermint gum.

"I'm dropping out of the competition," Vern announced.

Before anyone could say anything, the elevator pinged and the sound of many feet came rushing down the hall. "You say you have a rattler trapped under there?" the first security guard asked when they got to the door.

"Definitely," Joe answered, still keeping both hands on the garbage can.

"I'll take that over," another guard said. He put his hands next to Joe's, and Joe stepped back. "We have Wildlife Services on the way."

"We need you kids to clear out of here now," the first guard said. "Go down to the pool or the café until we get things under control."

We headed out into the hall. "You're really dropping out of the contest?" Douglas asked. He was talking to Vern but looking at the floor.

"I think this is a conversation we should be having with everyone in the group," said Angie. "Let's get Kyle and Jordan."

Ten minutes later we were sitting at a big table poolside. Tiki torches flickered around us. Vern finished filling in Kyle and Jordan on what had happened to him. "That's why I think I'm going to drop out of the competition. We've got one guy dead. And we've got two guys who almost died. Me and Jordan."

"The way I figure it, I've survived the worst," Jordan said. "Thanks to Frank and Joe, I didn't end up shark chow. I'm not quitting now. If I did, they might not let me stay for the Super Bowl, and my life's not worth living if I don't see the Super Bowl live once."

"I'm not quitting," Kyle spat out. "You know how much I gave up for this?" The torches threw shadows over his face, making him look like a stranger. "My girlfriend dumped me because I wasn't spending enough time with her. I gave up chess, even though I've competed in national tournaments. I haven't even watched any of the new season of *Lost*. I am absolutely not quitting. You all quit if you want. It's not like any of you are going to win anyway."

"So you care because you want to win? That's it?" Angie asked.

"What do you mean, that's it?" demanded Kyle.

"I mean, is that the only reason you care? Just so you'll be number one or whatever?"

"I trained for—"

"I get that. What you don't get is what I'm asking." Angie shoved her glasses higher on her nose and snapped her gum. "Look, I want to win, because I want the *money*. I want to go to NYU film school. My parents won't pay. They'll only pay if I go to college for something so-called practical. This is my shot to do what I want with my life. Do you get the difference? I'm talking about my life. I'm not quitting."

"Me either," Douglas said. He didn't give his reasons. But Joe and I already knew what they were. The journal had been way too clear.

"We're not quitters," Joe said for both of us.

"Are you idiots, then?" Vern demanded, flipping his bangs out of his face. "Are you all idiots? You can't win if you're dead. You can't go to film school if you're dead. You can't do anything if you're dead." He stood up so fast he knocked his chair over.

"Look, the contest is almost here. We're less than a day away," Angie said. "There's not much time for whoever's doing this garbage to do anything else." She got to her feet. "So what I'm going to do is go to my room. I'm eating dinner from room service. I'm going to stay in my room and away from all of you—because, sorry to say it, it seems like one of you is completely psycho and trying to kill the rest of us."

She turned around and started to walk away. "See you at the competition," she added over her shoulder.

Vern stared after her, then shook his head. "If you're all staying in, I guess I'm staying in too. Why should I be the only sane one?" He gave a shaky smile. "Besides, I've already had my turn. Maybe whoever's doing this will come after one of you next."

10.
Crazy and Insane

"What do you think? Will the killer make a play for somebody else before the competition?" I asked Frank. We were still sitting by the pool. Everyone else had gone up to their rooms. They'd all decided that Angie had the right idea to just lay low.

"Whoever the killer is, they're feeling desperate," Frank answered. "They tried to kill two people in less than a day. That's incredibly risky."

"I guess we can take Vern off our suspect list now that he's been a victim. At least as long as we're assuming the same person who killed David is also responsible for the attacks on Jordan and Vern," I said.

"I think we should keep that as our theory for now," Frank agreed. "So, yeah, Jordan and Vern are off our list unless something changes."

"So who is still on?" It helped to think out loud.

"Kyle and Douglas, even though we didn't find any evidence against them in their rooms," said Frank.

"Kyle has even more invested in the competition than we thought. Can you believe he lost his girlfriend over the amount of time he spent training?" I shook my head. "Actually, I can totally believe it," I said, answering my own question. "What I really meant was—isn't it insane that he was willing to lose his girlfriend over his crazy training routine?"

"Crazy and insane. Those are both words that could describe our killer, don't you think?" Frank asked. "Someone who is willing to take multiple lives to win a contest. A hot dog eating contest."

"Except we have to remember it's not necessarily just about winning the contest. It's about what winning the contest can bring. Like what Angie was saying. For her it's a chance to go to film school."

"That's still not a good reason to murder people," Frank protested.

"I'm not saying it is. I'm just saying it's not just about wanting to be the one who eats the most hot dogs," I told him. "Like Douglas. He clearly feels like he's not worth anything if he can't get some kind of trophy. He has this twisted idea that his parents will care more about him if he wins tomorrow."

"True." Frank stretched his arms up over his head. "So Kyle, Douglas, and Angie all have big reasons for wanting to win. How do we narrow that list down?"

"There's also the cute blond girl who's in the hotel and was at the competition when David was killed," I reminded him.

"I'm trying to make the list shorter, not longer," Frank complained. "But we definitely can't forget about her."

"At this point, I think it would be hard to get Angie out of her room for long enough to do a search. And we don't know which room the Mystery Girl is in," I said. I tapped my forehead with my fingers. Sometimes that jars ideas loose.

"That tapping thing never works," Frank told me.

"You don't know that." I kept tapping.

"Yeah, I do. Because I've seen you tapping. And then I've seen the lack of ideas that follows."

"Maybe the ideas do follow. Maybe they just don't follow at the speed you expect them to. Since you don't have a little surveillance camera in my brain, you can't be sure." I kept tapping, even though it was making my forehead sore and I wanted to stop. Sometimes a big brother with his big-brother attitude can do that to you.

"Surveillance camera," Frank repeated. He

jumped up. "There isn't one in your head, but they are all over this hotel. We need to see what they got of the hall outside Vern's room."

"Right! Because that snake didn't wiggle up sixteen floors by itself. And it wasn't tall enough to reach the buttons on the elevator." I stood up too. "One problem. Hotel security isn't just going to hand over the tape to two kids."

"Tape. Who are you, Dad?" Frank asked. "This hotel is part of an exclusive top-of-the-line chain. All their security stuff has to be stored on a hard drive. And I'm betting that the files are also all sent to a main office."

"Got it," I said. I grabbed my cell and punched in Vijay Patel's number. Vijay is with ATAC too. He's working at getting undercover assignments, but for right now, he handles various kinds of backup. Like delivering "game cartridges." And hacking.

"Vij," I said when he picked up. "Frank and I need some info that is probably out in the ethernet between two branches of the Coconut Oasis Hotel chain."

"When is somebody going to come up with something challenging for me to do?" he complained.

"I wish somebody would," I answered. "I think you have a little too much time for Christmas shopping."

I had a pretty good idea who thought those Underoos were funny.

"Hey, I don't do Christmas. I'm a Hindu. Born in India and everything," Vijay reminded me. But I could hear in his voice that he was trying not to crack up. I could also hear that he was already clacking away at his computer keyboard.

"He's on it," I told Frank. "What's the plan?" I asked Vijay.

"I'm just going to run a few remote exploits until I'm allowed unauthorized data access and the Coconut website starts telling me all kinds of secrets it shouldn't," Vijay said.

"What kind of exploits?" I'd been wanting to take one of ATAC's extensive hacking training sessions. But with school and missions, there hadn't been time.

"I'm going to make it do math that's too hard. Computers go crazy if they try to create a numeric value that's too big for the available storage space," Vijay answered. "I'm going to give it a piece of data that's too big to handle. That'll make it overwrite some metadata, which will let me overwrite a little data of my own. And, oooh, they have a guest book on the site. That's always a nice place to inject a piece of code. You'd think a few lines of space to write 'Hi there, loved your hotel' would be harmless. But you'd be wrong."

Frank tapped me on the arm and raised his eyebrows.

"He's doing . . . stuff," I told him.

"And I'm in. That was too easy," said Vijay. "I was just starting to have fun, and it cracked open like an egg. Now what exactly do you need?"

"Security footage. From today. Sixteenth floor of the Miami hotel," I told him.

"I'll get it to your laptop ASAP," Vijay promised.

Frank shut the laptop. "That gave us nothing."

"And after Vijay got his guru on," I said.

We'd isolated the footage of Vern's door and watched it. We'd fast-forwarded through every minute since Vern checked in, slowing down to regular speed any time anybody was close to his room. My eyes felt as dry as cotton balls. But we hadn't seen anything useful.

No one had gone into Vern's room since he arrived, except Vern. Not until Angie, Frank, and I ran in there after he screamed. He'd kept the DO NOT DISTURB sign on his door the whole time. That meant not even one of the maids had gone in.

I was about to start tapping on my forehead again when Frank said, "Wait."

"What?" I asked, my hands halfway to my head.

"The front door isn't the only way in to the room. We should know that better than anyone," said Frank.

I got it. "The balcony."

Frank leaned forward. "Yeah. Maybe we weren't the only ones climbing around out there today."

"We pretty much know we weren't, actually," I said. "We know the Mystery Girl was on Angie's balcony. We didn't mess that up. We were on the balcony right next to Douglas's. And Angie's room is right next to his."

"But Angie had no idea who we were talking about when we described the Mystery Girl to her, even though she came out of Angie's room."

"Maybe she was moving along the balconies and saw us coming. So maybe she just pretended Angie's room was hers," I suggested. "We didn't see her come out of there. She could have already been on the balcony. In the shadows."

"Makes sense to me. And now that we know no one went into Vern's room through the front door, the Mystery Girl is at the very top of our suspect list," Frank announced.

"We've got to find her," I said.

"Fast," Frank agreed. "Before she has the chance to go after anyone else."

11.
The Secret Identity of Mystery Girl

Joe and I stared at each other. "So how are we supposed to do this extremely fast finding?" he asked.

I tapped my fingers lightly on my keyboard. It's my version of Joe's forehead tapping. "Well, when you want to find a lost dog, you put up posters with a picture on them. And lost kids get their pictures on milk cartons."

"The Sketch program," Joe said, just as I was clicking on the icon.

"Face shape first. Round, oval, triangle, inverted triangle, or square?" I asked.

Joe studied the outlines of the basic faces. "It's hard. Her face on the YouTube clip was really small, and she was mostly in shadow on the balcony. But I'm thinking inverted triangle. She had one of those cute pointy chins, didn't you think?"

I should be good at remembering faces. It's part of being a good detective and ATAC agent. And usually I can recall every mole and line. It's just with a certain kind of subject . . .

"Sorry, forgot we were talking teenage girl," Joe said. "Your Kryptonite. So use the inverted triangle."

I clicked on it and brought up a selection of eye shapes. Joe frowned at them. "Go with those."

I selected the wide-set eyes, with the somewhat hooded lids, and we moved on to lips. Joe had way too many more words of description for those than I needed. "You're forgetting the *fast* part of extremely fast finding," I told him.

"Okay, those." He tapped the screen. "With that awesome full perfect curvy part on top. Too bad there's not a way to put an accent on the screen. I thought her accent was cool."

I shook my head as I clicked the lips. We ran through eyebrows and noses. Joe chose brows that were "kind of pointy, but not Jack Nicholson scary pointy," and a nose that was "Ashlee Simpson pre-surgery." He had problems with the cheekbones, so we tried four in the face we'd been creating, and he finally chose a fairly narrow pair. We skipped ears, because her long hair had covered them, but we played around with the hairline for a few minutes. Different hairlines really change the face shape.

"What do you think?" I asked Joe when our most current version came up on the screen.

"I think if you'd seen the Mystery Girl, you'd recognize her from this picture," he said. "At least I hope."

"Let's give it a shot." I faxed the picture to the front desk. Then we rushed to the lobby to pick it up.

"Have you seen this girl in the hotel?" Joe asked the tall guy—oval face, straight brows, wide cheekbones, eagle nose, small mouth, receding hairline—when he got the fax for us. See, I am good with facial details when I'm not in my trouble area.

The guy eyed the computer-generated sketch for a moment. "Sorry. Can't say I have."

"Anybody else?" Joe called. He held the sketch up so everyone working behind the registration desk could see it. "Does she look familiar to any of you?"

We got a variety of ways to express no. We headed to the concierge desk. Got a "nope." We circled the lobby, checking with all the guests, except the ones who were in line to check in. More no's.

We checked with the people poolside—both indoor and outdoor pools. Nothing and nothing.

"Man, this is getting to be like washing your hair," Joe muttered.

"What?" I figured I'd heard him wrong.

"You know. Lather, rinse, and repeat," explained Joe.

I must have still looked like I had no idea what he was talking about. "The instructions on the shampoo bottle," he said. "I thought you read the instructions for everything. I know I saw you reading the instructions for opening the milk carton the other day."

This was another one of those times where Joe just has to be ignored. "I think we should try the maids and the room service people," I told him. "They see a lot of hotel guests."

It was true. They did. But none of them we talked to remembered seeing the Mystery Girl. "The gym?" I suggested.

"We don't have any other leads," Joe said. "We might as well keep showing the sketch around."

The gym was feeling pointless when we'd worked through the free-weight section, three Stair-Masters, and two elliptical trainers of no's. Then we hit the Lifecycles. First one, we got a hit.

"Isn't that Savannah Harris?" the woman riding

the bike to nowhere said, a little breathless.

"Who?" I asked.

"Savannah—I think that's her name. Maybe Cheyenne? But definitely Harris. She's the daughter of this big money guy who lives in Atlanta. That's where I'm from. She's always in the paper there."

Atlanta. That matched up with Mystery Girl's Southern accent.

"Thanks," Joe told her. "That was a big help."

Joe and I rushed back to our room and got back on the laptop. When you're an ATAC agent and you're not in the middle of fighting a forest fire or a shark, you're on the computer. I typed the name "Savannah Harris" into the Google search bar.

"She seems to be somebody," Joe commented, checking out the number of hits.

I clicked on the first link. The article that opened—a short little piece from an Atlanta gossip column—had a picture of a girl with long blond hair, wide-set eyes, pointy eyebrows. I glanced over at Joe. He'd gotten a better look at the Mystery Girl . . . for reasons I don't need to go into again.

"I'm not a hundred percent positive. The dress doesn't show the bumblebee tattoo. But I'm ninety percent," he told me. "So what's her deal?"

"Sixteen-year-old Savannah Harris, daughter of

Matthias Harris, helps out at the DAR's silent auction to raise money to fight world hunger," I said, reading the caption under the photo. I hit another link. There was another photo of Savannah. This time the bumblebee had made the picture. So had Savannah's dad.

"Mystery girl—I mean Savannah Harris—just got motive," Joe burst out. He pointed to the words "Matthias Harris, owner of the multinational company Stadium Franks" in the middle of the new article.

I nodded. "Right. Her father's company is in competition with Football Franks. Bad publicity for the contest equals bad publicity for her father's competitor."

"And dead people—or even just canceled competitions—that's what I'd call bad publicity," said Joe. "Is there something higher than the top of the suspect list? Because if there is, Savannah Harris should be up there."

"Agreed," I said. "The only problem is, even though we know who the Mystery Girl is now, we still don't know where she is."

"Let's check with the front desk, just in case she's staying here and registered under her own name," Joe suggested.

A couple of minutes later, we were back in

front of the tall, oval-faced, straight-browed,
wide-cheek-boned, eagle-nosed, small-mouthed,
receding-hairlined desk clerk. "Hello again," he
said. "Expecting another fax?"

"No," I told him. "We just wanted to see if a friend of ours is checked in. Savannah Harris."

The clerk clicked a few keys on his computer. "We have no one by that name registered."

"Thanks anyway," Joe said.

"Just a minute," the clerk called as we turned away. "Let me get you some club soda. It should get that stain on your sleeve right out." He hurried off.

Joe glanced at the splotch on his sleeve. "Didn't even know it was there." He brushed at it, then glanced at his fingers. "This stuff is funky-looking. What do you think it even is?" he asked me.

He held his hand up in front of my face. The gunk on his fingers was tan and bumpy. I shook my head. "I don't know. It looks like your fingers are breaking out."

"There's no way I'm getting zits on my hands," Joe said. He rubbed his fingers together. The bumps collapsed and smeared. He frowned, then wiped his hand on his shirt.

I winced. Joe can be such a slob.

"What?" he asked. "It had that gunk on it already."

"Here you go," the clerk said, returning with the club soda. He didn't know my brother. Joe's only method of stain removal is his own spit, if he even bothers to try that.

"Thanks," Joe told him.

"I don't have any idea what to do next," I admitted as we headed away from the desk.

"Me either." Joe flopped down on one of the pale green sofas in a corner of the lobby away from everybody else. I snagged the chair across from him.

"I hate to admit it, but I wouldn't mind hearing Dad's advice right about now," I said.

Joe pointed at me. "You are never going to let him know those words came out of your mouth. And anyway, we both know what he'd say. He's given us every piece of advice he has about a hundred times."

"So give it to me. What would he say?" I asked.

"If you're at a dead end, go back to the beginning," Joe told me.

I leaned my head back and stared up at the ceiling. "The beginning. We got the game cartridge with the mission on it in the box of Underoos."

"That's a little too much detail," said Joe. "There are some things I'd like to forget."

"You never know which details are important. That's another thing Dad's told us a hundred times," I reminded him.

"Okay, okay, so we got the deets on David Cole's death. It was murder. And we got assigned to go undercover as gurgitators. We did some research, did a little practicing, arrived here. You wouldn't let me hit the pool. You had me do more research. We gathered info on the other contestants."

I lifted my head up so I could look at him. "You left out the part about the death threats," I said. "Then we went to dinner. We met Jordan. Who seemed a lot more interested in football than—"

"Anything else in life," Joe finished for me.

"Definitely more interested in the Super Bowl than in the contest," I agreed. I concentrated on getting the sequence of events right. "Then Kyle showed."

"Frank Hardy!" Joe said, doing the Kyle Skloot finger point at me.

"Yeah. He made himself real popular, bragging about how hard he'd trained and how he was absolutely going to win," I continued.

"Angie and Douglas were next up." Joe was counting off the contestants on his fingers. "Douglas hardly said anything."

"And Angie went after Kyle, remember?" I asked.

"It was great!" Joe answered. "She was all, 'You wouldn't even be here if that other guy hadn't died.' And she kept snapping her gum at him."

"That mix of watermelon and peppermint," I said. "I could smell it from where I was sitting."

"Say that again," Joe demanded.

"What? Watermelon and peppermint?" I shrugged. "It is a weird combination. But no weirder than some of the food other people were combining that night. I was eating oatmeal and cabbage myself."

"Watermelon and peppermint. Fruity and spicy. That's how the Mystery Girl smelled to me when we were talking to her on the balcony," Joe told me. "That's kind of bizarre. Like you said, it's a weird combination."

"She was on Angie's balcony," I said slowly. "Angie's the other one with the smell. But I don't get what that could mean."

"Do you think they know each other?" Joe asked. "Do you think that room is really Mystery Girl's—I mean Savannah's—and Angie's? If you share a room, it's normal that you'd share packs of gum." He paused. "Could they be working together?" Joe's eyes began flicking back and forth, the way they do when his brain is piecing together connections.

"What would Angie's motive be for that? Savannah wants bad publicity for the competition, because bad publicity for Football Franks is good publicity for her father's company. And bad publicity on TV during the Super Bowl—that's a lot of bad publicity. More people watch the Super Bowl than almost anything else," I said. "But Angie just wants to win the contest and go to film school."

"Doesn't seem like their motives go together. One wants to pretty much bring the contest down. One wants to win it. If we have their motives straight," agreed Joe.

"But the weird smell thing, and Savannah being on Angie's balcony . . . I'm not ready to let that go," I admitted.

"Why don't we go show our drawing of Savannah to Angie?" Joe suggested. "When we described Savannah to her, she said she hadn't seen anyone like that. But I'd be curious to see her reaction if we stick the sketch in front of her face and use the name Savannah Harris."

"Can't hurt. And we've got nothing else to go on right now." I got up, and we took another ride in the glass elevator.

Joe gave a couple of loud knocks on Angie's door.

No answer.

Not even a whisper of movement from inside.

"That's strange." Joe tried the door. Locked.

"Angie said she was going to stay in her room all night. She sounded like she was too scared to go out for anything."

I knocked on the door. "Angie!" I called. "Are you okay?"

"She might be pretending she's not there because she thinks anyone in the contest—including us— could be the killer," said Joe. "I don't know why I thought she'd just open up to look at the picture."

"Or maybe she's in there, but the killer's already gotten to her." I pulled the lock pick out of my pocket. A few twists, a jerk, and the door swung open.

Angie lay on the floor. A bowl of salad, two apples, and some carrots were scattered next to her.

"I don't think she's breathing," Joe said.

12.
She's Not Breathing

I dashed over to Angie and dropped to my knees next to her. I pressed my ear to her chest. It felt . . . bulky. Bunchy. I couldn't tell if she was breathing or not.

I realized her sweatshirt had a layer of padding sewn into it. Another technique to sweat without burning calories? Didn't matter right now. I ripped out as much of the padding as I could and pressed my head to her chest again.

She definitely wasn't breathing.

Airway. First I needed to clear the airway. Gently I tilted her chin up. That made her head fall backward. Her glasses fell off, and I pushed them aside. Okay, now with her head back, air should be able to flow into her nose and mouth.

But I didn't see her chest rising and falling. And I should be able to tell now that the padding was gone.

I brought my ear close to her lips, getting a whiff of that mint and watermelon. I listened for inhaling and exhaling.

Nothing.

"She's not breathing," I yelled to Frank.

"Check her pulse. I'll call 911." He scrambled for the phone. I pressed my fingers against Angie's throat. For a moment, all I could feel was my own wild heartbeat pounding through my body. I took a deep breath. Focused.

"She's got a pulse," I told Frank. "Erratic, but there."

"Start rescue breathing," he said.

I nodded. We'd both had serious EMT training through ATAC. I made sure Angie's head was still tilted back, then I pinched her nose closed with my thumb and index finger. *Breathe slow*, I coached myself as I pressed my mouth over Angie's. As my breath entered her, I watched to see if her chest rose. It didn't.

That was bad.

Okay, retilt the head, try again. I angled Angie's chin back, then clamped my mouth over hers and breathed out.

115

Her chest didn't rise.

That was very bad.

"They're on the way," Frank said, dropping down next to me. "What's happening?"

"The air's not getting to her," I answered.

Frank kept staring at me.

"The air's not getting to her," I repeated, sure he hadn't heard me.

"No, it's not that. I just realized that stuff that was on your shirt. He reached out and swiped his finger over the skin by the side of my mouth. It came away tan and bumpy. "This came off Angie's face. It's not acne. It's makeup."

I stared back down at Angie—who I'd thought was Angie. There were patches of clear skin on her face now. My eyes flicked from them to the padding strewn over the floor. Suddenly my heart began to race as it hit me—I couldn't believe I hadn't put it together before now. "This isn't Angie. I don't know if there even is an Angie. I think it's Savannah."

"I think you're right," Frank agreed. "But right now, let's just get her breathing." He leaned closer to—the girl. "The angle on her head is good. But Joe, look how swollen her tongue is. That's why she can't get air."

Frank was right. Her tongue hardly fit in her

mouth anymore. "Let me try her nose." I covered the girl's nose with my lips, getting a mouth full of makeup. Then I breathed out slowly.

Her chest didn't rise.

"What's going on? The swollen tongue shouldn't be keeping the air from getting to her lungs now." Frustration and fear raced through me.

Frank picked a leaf out of the salad on the floor and rubbed it between his fingers.

"What are you doing?" I demanded.

"This is elephant ear. It's poisonous," Frank said. "In extreme cases it can cause the throat to swell."

That was it, then. Her throat was too swollen to let the air travel through. "We have no idea how long she's been oxygen-deprived," I said. "I don't know if we can risk waiting for the EMTs to get here."

"We know the procedure," Frank noted, his face grim. "We've practiced it dozens of times."

On dummies. I didn't speak the thought out loud.

"I'll see if there's any disinfectant in the bathroom." I shoved myself to my feet and hurried in there. I didn't see any disinfectant, but I spotted some astringent. Better than nothing. I grabbed the bottle, and all the clean hand towels.

When I ran back to the girl's side, I saw that Frank had removed a short brown wig from the girl. Long, sweat-soaked blond hair now tumbled around her face.

"It's definitely Savannah Harris," said Frank as I swabbed her neck with the astringent. "She's wearing colored contacts—brown ones."

"Yeah," I said. "Her eyes were blue in the pictures. She's been disguising herself as Angie."

"We'll have to deal with it later. Do you have your Swiss Army knife?" Frank asked.

I took it out of my pocket and wiped the largest blade down with the astringent. "What are we going to use for a tube?" I asked. I kept glancing at the door. All I wanted was to see the EMTs running in. All I wanted was for us not to have to do this.

"Straw from the sports bottle!" exclaimed Frank. He reached up and grabbed a lime green sports bottle off the dresser. He pulled the large, hard plastic straw out and disinfected it with the astringent. Then he poured some of the astringent over both our hands. "Do you remember how to find the trachea?"

EMTs, EMTs, where are they? I shot a look at the door, then returned all my attention to Angie's throat. I kept thinking of her as Angie, even though

118

we'd figured out that Angie had just been a disguise of Savannah's.

"I feel for where the collarbones meet," I said, pressing my fingers against Angie's neck as I talked. "Then above that I'll feel the trachea."

"Right, now you just need a cut about a half an inch across it," Frank coached.

I didn't look for the EMTs. I didn't let my eyes waver from the spot I'd identified as Angie's trachea. Carefully, but quickly, I made the cut. Frank slid his finger in it to keep it open. Then he moved the hard plastic straw into the hole.

Moment-of-truth time.

I leaned down and breathed two puffs of air into the straw. Frank and I stared at Angie's chest.

It rose.

Frank and I grinned at each other. "She's breathing," I said. I knew he could see that she was. But I wanted to say it.

I looked down at Angie. "You're going to be okay, Angie. Savannah, I mean." She was still unconscious, but I wanted to say that, too. I touched her shoulder. "More padding," I told Frank. "She really went all out for the disguise."

"She was good, too. Not even a trace of her Southern accent came through," Frank added.

I just watched her breathe then. I felt like I

could watch that for a very long time without getting bored. But I didn't get the chance.

The EMTs arrived, rolling a gurney into the room. "We couldn't get her breathing with mouth-to-mouth. We didn't know how long she'd been without air, so we thought we had to do an emergency tracheotomy," Frank explained as they prepped her for the ambulance.

"You thought right," one of the EMTs answered, flipping her long braid over her shoulder.

I picked up the piece of elephant ear leaf off the floor. "My brother figured out this is what she ate. What poisoned her. We're not sure how much she got down."

"It's called elephant ear," said Frank.

The other EMT took the leaf from me. "The docs will want to take a look at it. What's this girl's name?"

"Savannah Harris," Frank answered. "Her parents aren't here. They're in Atlanta. But we'll call them."

"Tell them we're taking her to Mercy Hospital," the EMT with the braid said. Then they rolled Savannah—I was getting the Savannah part in my head—out of the room.

Frank and I finally got back to our own room. We'd had to answer a bunch of questions from the hotel manager about exactly what had happened. We left out the part with the lock pick and the double identity and just said we were friends with Angie, and we got worried when she didn't open the door. It was unlocked, so we went in, and she wasn't breathing.

We explained that we'd both taken a lifeguarding class that involved a lot of first aid, and that's how we'd known how to do the emergency tracheotomy.

I still couldn't believe I'd made a cut into someone's throat. As I flopped back on my bed, I realized that the back of my shirt was glued to me with my own sweat. If you want to know all the gory details, the pits of the shirt were soaked too, and I didn't exactly smell like a daisy.

"We've gotta call Savannah's parents," Frank said.

I moaned. I knew he was right, but that's not a conversation you want to have. "You do it," I told him. "You're the older one."

"I'll flip you for it." Frank sat down on his bed and picked up a quarter from the nightstand. "Heads or tails?"

"Tails," I told him. "No, wait. Remember that article you were telling me about? The one that said that there's a flaw in the coin flip?"

"Oh, yeah. It said that a coin is always more likely to land on the same side it starts out on," Frank said.

"So coin tosses are bogus. Let's do rock, paper, scissors." I threw my choice. I lost.

I sucked in a deep breath, sat up, and dialed information. There was a number for Matthias Harris in Atlanta listed. Just one number. I checked the clock. Nine thirty. At least I probably wouldn't be waking anybody up.

I punched in the number and waited while it rang. A man answered. "I'd like to speak to Mr. Matthias Harris, please," I said.

"This is," he told me.

"Mr. Harris, my name is Joe Hardy. I'm a friend of your daughter's. She's all right, but she's been taken to the hospital. She accidentally ingested some poison." Accidentally in that she didn't mean to eat poison. Not in the way that somebody had tried to kill her. Mr. Harrison could get that info after he'd had time to absorb the first part.

"What? How did it happen?" Mr. Harris exclaimed. "Never mind," he said before I could answer. "Where is she?"

"She's at Mercy Hospital in Miami."

"That's impossible. My daughter was spending the weekend two blocks away from here at her cousin's," he shot back. "Are you sure you have the right person? My daughter is Savannah Harris."

"Savannah Harris, yes. I don't know what she told you, but she's been in Miami since at least Friday," I answered.

"What is she doing there?"

It really didn't sound like he knew. If Savannah was sabotaging the Football Franks competition to help her dad, it wasn't because he asked her to.

"What is she doing there? And who are you again?" Mr. Harris demanded.

"Joe Hardy. I'm here to enter the Football Franks Hot Dog Eating Contest. Your daughter was in the contest too."

Frank leaned closer. I knew he wished he could hear what Mr. Harris had to say to that.

"That contest of Edward's that's giving out college money?" Mr. Harris burst out.

"Yes, that's it," I answered.

"Film school," said Mr. Harris, sounding angry, and disgusted, and scared out of his head. "This is all because I said I wouldn't pay for film school."

Film school? I'd figured that was part of Savannah's cover story. I thought it was as fake as Angie's acne.

"The winner does get scholarship money, am

123

I right?" Mr. Harris continued. "I've seen all the commercials."

"It could be over three hundred thousand dollars for school," I answered.

"If I'd known she wanted it that bad . . . We'll have to talk about it. But why am I wasting time on it now?" Mr. Harris said, clearly talking to himself a lot more than he was talking to me. "Mercy Hospital, you said? Miami?"

"Right."

"Her mother and I will be on the next available flight. No, we'll charter a plane." His voice cracked on the last word. It was like all the news was finally hitting him. "She's really all right?"

"She had to have an emergency tracheotomy, but she should be fine," I assured him. I didn't tell him that the procedure had been performed by two teenage guys. He didn't need to be picturing that the whole flight to Florida.

"We'll be there soon. Thank you for calling us."

"Wow," I said when I hung up. "That was intense. And that thing that Angie-slash-Savannah said about wanting to win the contest so she could get money for film school because her parents wouldn't pay? It seems like that part is true."

"Now that she's become a victim too, it doesn't make much sense that she was behind the other attacks and David's murder," Frank pointed out.

"Yeah. She's off the suspect list for the same reason Vern and Jordan are. Who'd put themselves in extreme danger to throw off suspicion? If we'd broken into Savannah's room a few minutes later . . ." I didn't want to actually say what could have happened.

"So we're down to Douglas and Kyle again," Frank said.

"They both have motive. They both have opportunity. But we haven't found any evidence against either of them." I rubbed my face with my hands, and my fingers came away with some of the makeup Savannah had used to give herself—or Angie's self—bad skin. "I just realized how this gunk got on my shirt!" I exclaimed. "Savannah's cheek must have brushed against my sleeve when we were dealing with the snake. She was right next to me."

"Why do you think she was at the L.A. contest—since we don't think she was there to kill David?" Frank asked.

"Maybe just to get some intel. Watch the competition's techniques. She really wanted to win," I suggested.

"I guess," Frank said. "Well, Kyle or Douglas—whichever one is the killer—has managed to eliminate one person from the competition. There's no way Savannah's going to be eating anything but hospital food tomorrow."

"Yeah," I agreed. "And they got rid of David, who would probably have been the guy to beat, no matter what Kyle says."

"Do you think that's enough for whoever the murderer is?"

I wanted to say "definitely."

"I don't know," I admitted.

"There haven't been any attempts on us yet," Frank reminded me. Like I needed a reminder of that. "Maybe the killer will try something before the contest. We could catch them in the act. That would give us all the evidence we need."

"If we don't die," I joked.

Frank's right. Sometimes the only thing you can do is ignore me.

13.

The Super Bowl of Hot Dog Eating

I sat in the hardest chair in the room, working away at my fifth energy drink. It wasn't doing much for me. You'd think the fact that I was on guard against the possibility of getting murdered would be keeping me hyperalert. And it did, on my first shift.

But this was my last. My eyes were burning. I was even starting to do that head-jerk thing, where you kind of fall asleep without realizing it, and your head droops, then snaps back up.

It had been quiet all night. Neither Kyle nor Douglas—or whoever the murderer was—had made a move toward me and Joe. In less than a day, our suspects would be heading home, off to different states. Joe and I had to get it together and

127

find some evidence, or we might end up letting a killer walk. And that was unacceptable.

My brain felt like it was pulsing. Were we missing something? That Angie-is-Savannah revelation had been a shocker. Why hadn't I noticed she was wearing a wig? Or wondered why her body was pudgy but her face wasn't?

Because she's in your teen girl blind spot, I answered myself. I had to work on that.

I checked the clock. Then I gave the bottom of my brother's bed a kick. "Joe, get up. It's almost time to go downstairs for breakfast with the guys."

Joe rolled over. "Not possible. I've been asleep for ten minutes."

"You've been asleep for two hours," I told him. "Come on. Up."

He grabbed his pillow and put it over his head. "Whatever," I said. "I'm taking a shower. If you're still in bed when I get out, it's the Aunt Trudy method for you."

Joe didn't answer. I left him sleeping, took a fast shower, brushed my teeth, then filled a glass of water from the sink. I smiled as I headed back over to Joe and held the glass over his head. "Wakey-wakey, eggs and bakey," I cooed, doing my Aunt Trudy. "This is your final warning," I added, switching back over to my voice.

Joe didn't twitch. So I pulled the pillow off his head and dumped the water over him.

"Oh, man. That was not cool," he complained.

"You have to work on the speed of your wake-up," I told him. "If there had been an incident with the killer—"

"You know I would have been on my feet in a second," Joe interrupted.

"Have you forgotten that the killer might be sitting at the breakfast table right now?" I asked as I got dressed.

Joe started pulling on his own clothes.

"You're not taking a shower?"

"You're the one who just said the killer might be sitting at the breakfast table right now," Joe reminded me. "I know being neat and clean is more important to you than almost anything, but I have different priorities."

"At least brush your teeth, swamp breath," I politely suggested.

Joe gave me a you-are-not-my-mother look. But a minute later I heard teeth-brushing sounds from the bathroom. If he didn't brush his hair, I wasn't going to say anything. But the lack of teeth brushing affected me, too. I had to smell him.

"Are you ready?" Joe asked when he stepped

out of the bathroom. "I'm always waiting for you. Gosh!"

I cracked up. Joe does a really good Napoleon Dynamite.

Maybe I should make him do it again, I thought when we arrived at our table in the restaurant. Jordan and Kyle were already there, and they looked like they could use a laugh.

"Did you guys know Angie got poisoned last night?" asked Kyle.

"Yeah," I said.

"How'd you find out?" Joe said. Excellent question. Did Kyle know because he was the one who put the elephant ear in her salad?

"I was coming into the lobby when the EMTs were wheeling her out," Kyle answered.

"So is that it, do you think?" asked Jordan. "Whoever is doing this got somebody out of the competition. There's no way Angie's going to be there. Is that enough for them now? David's gone. Angie's gone. Is that enough?" His voice got louder and louder. He pretty much yelled the last question. Good thing they'd put us in a private room, which they'd probably done because they'd figured out our mass food consumption wasn't that pleasant to watch.

"If they wanted to win, they would have had to kill me," Kyle said.

That was his usual bragging style. But it didn't have quite the swagger behind it that it usually did. Huh. I wondered how Douglas would be acting this morning.

"You're such an idiot," Vern said. He'd arrived in time to hear Kyle. "A person actually died. Other people almost died. Do you even listen to yourself when you talk?"

"All I was saying was, if somebody wants to win so badly they're murdering people, they should be going after the toughest competitor. And that wasn't Angie," Kyle explained.

"Angie? What does Angie have to do with it?" asked Vern as Douglas joined the group.

"You don't know?" Kyle said.

"I've been locked in my room since I saw you guys yesterday," Vern said. "It sounded like a good idea when Angie said it."

"Somebody tried to poison Angie last night," Joe told him. "She's in the hospital, but she's going to be okay."

Vern put his face in his hands for a long moment. Then he raised his head and looked at each person sitting at the table. "One of us did it to her, right? It has to have been one of us?"

"Attempts to kill—or at least hurt—you and Jordan were made too. The only connection you, Jordan, and Angie have is the competition, right?" I asked.

"We may as well add David Cole in there too," added Joe.

"Fine. And David. Was there another connection among the four of you?" If there was, that would take our case in a whole different direction.

"I never met Angie or Jordan before Friday. Never talked to them or anything," Vern said. "And I never met David Cole. I knew who they all were, because of the contest, but that's it."

I looked over at Jordan. He gave a helpless shrug. "Same for me."

"Then it seems like the only thing the victims have in common is the eating contest. And it seems like the only motive is reducing the competition. Or am I missing something?" I looked around the table. "Can anyone else think of anything?"

No one said anything. I turned to Vern. "Then I guess you're probably right. The only people who could benefit from Angie getting poisoned, and all the other stuff, are all of us sitting here."

"But it's over, right?" Jordan asked again.

"It's not over until the contest is over," Kyle shot back. "Do you have the memory of a goldfish or something? David Cole died practically in the middle of the contest. That could happen to one of us today."

"Then why are we even doing this?" exclaimed Vern.

"Don't start with that again," Kyle told him. "All I care about is who has been doing this to us. I know it's not me. You and you got attacked"—he pointed to Jordan and Vern—"so I figure you're both out."

Kyle stood up and began to pace around the table. Like he was playing some extreme version of duck, duck, goose. "That leaves you." He paused behind me. "You." He paused behind Joe. "And you." He stopped behind Douglas and put both hands on Douglas's shoulders. I could see him digging his fingers in.

"Now, this guy seems like too much of a wimp to kill anything, right?" Kyle asked. "Maybe a fly or something, but that's about it." He jerked his chin toward me and Joe. "Those two look more like the type who could figure out how to kill someone if they wanted to."

Joe and I exchanged a what's-going-on glance. Kyle kept on ranting. "But my money is still on this guy. Let's not forget, he was in L.A. when David was killed." Douglas tried to get to his feet, but Kyle held him in place.

I wasn't going to let this get too out of control. But I wanted to see it play out a little further. Maybe Joe and I could learn something about Kyle or Douglas that was vital.

"And you know how it is with killers. Their neighbors and the people who work with them and everyone are always saying that they were so surprised because the psycho seemed so nice and quiet," Kyle continued. "Now, doesn't that just about describe our friend Douglas here?"

"You're the one who's acting psycho," said Jordan.

"You want to win bad, don't you, Dougie?" Kyle asked. "I saw your sister prancing around yesterday, getting all the attention. I know that had to burn you. You want to show her that she's not so special, am I right?"

"Yes!" Douglas shouted. "I hate her. I hate how she's always dragging home trophies. She thinks she's so much better than me."

I heard Vern suck in his breath with a hiss.

Douglas gave a vicious twist and managed to get away from Kyle and onto his feet. He faced off with Kyle. "I do want to win. I want to show everyone I'm not nothing. But I didn't kill anyone."

Kyle crossed his arms over his chest. "I don't believe you. In fact, I'm even more convinced you're the killer after your little tantrum. So why don't we go find Mr. Poplin? You can confess everything, and then you can go take a nap in a place with nice, soft walls. And the rest of us can compete without worrying about being offed."

"Is it true, Douglas?" Jordan asked.

"It's obviously true," Kyle answered for him. He reached for Douglas's arm. Douglas shoved him back—hard. I sprang to my feet.

"You were in L.A. too," Douglas spat. "You're trying to turn this all around on me, but you were sitting right next to David when he died." He gave Kyle another push. "And you're the pathetic one. You had this great life. You had a girlfriend. You had friends. You probably even have some trophies for your chess. And you gave it all up so you could eat a lot of hot dogs. You're the psycho." He started to push Kyle again.

Kyle hauled back his fist. I was there before he could use it to smash Douglas's face in. I kept Kyle's arm pressed behind his back. "You don't have any proof of what you're saying, do you?" I asked.

Douglas shook his head. I looked around the table. "None of us knows who's behind the attacks, am I right?"

"I wish I did, but no," said Jordan.

"No," Douglas said, his voice back to its usual softness.

Joe and Vern shook their heads.

"Kyle?" I asked.

"Fine. I don't have proof," he muttered. I let him go and he sat down. I got back in my seat too.

"Hey, guys, we're going to the Super Bowl," Jordan called out. "Woo-hoo!" But his voice was flat, and I could tell he was scared. We all were.

Make that all but one. The murderer was still in control. What did he have to be afraid of?

That's going to change, I promised myself. *I'm not sure exactly how. But the killer is going to be the one feeling fear before this day is over.*

Second quarter. Fourth down, with two yards to go. Close game. The kind of game that could become legendary.

And our seats. Front row. *Front row* at the Super Bowl. You could hear the bones crunch. You could smell the sweat.

But Joe and I could hardly enjoy it. We were on high alert. There wasn't much time left if the killer planned to make another move. We had to be ready.

I scanned our group again. Jordan seemed out of his mind—with joy. I don't think I've ever seen a person as happy as he was right now. Once when I was at the park, I saw this woman open a brand-new can of tennis balls and give all three to her golden retriever at once. That golden retriever might have been as out-of-its-head happy as Jordan was right this second. Maybe.

Vern was hardly watching the game. Most of his attention was on working his way through two gallons of aloe vera juice.

Kyle wasn't watching the game at all. His eyes were closed, his hands palms up on his thighs. The guy was meditating. During the Super Bowl.

"I have to go to the bathroom," Vern announced.

"Me too," said Joe, following Vern out of our row, with a longing look toward the field. We'd agreed that none of our suspects was going anywhere unescorted. We didn't want any of them to have a chance to get near where the food was being prepped.

There were three of them, and only two of us, but it wasn't the kind of situation where the group really split up much. By the time Joe and Vern got back, the people running the contest wanted us in the locker room getting ready.

How cool is that? We got to use the home locker room. It was painted turquoise. It had a carpet with a huge dolphin wearing a football helmet on it. And it smelled . . . exactly like locker rooms always smell. Jordan was sucking in such deep breaths of the odor I started to think he might hyperventilate.

"Man, I'm lovin' this," he gasped.

"Okay, kids, it's almost show time," Mr. Poplin announced. "Here's Tommy the Tiger, Miami's most popular DJ. He'll be hosting."

A massive guy who looked like he could be a football player himself gave us a wave. "Nobody puke on me!" he warned with a smile.

"And you'll each have three of the Dolphins cheerleaders rooting you on," Mr. Poplin continued. "The blimp will be overhead flashing the number of dogs you've eaten. The counters will be radioing them up." He smiled. "And it will also be flashing the Football Franks logo, of course. We'll start things up—"

He was drowned out by the thundering sound of the Patriots returning to the locker room. Up close, it was almost like they were a different species.

"We'll get out of your way," Mr. Poplin called. "Kids, line up by the door where we came in. Tony's going to call your names one by one, and you'll run out to the table that's going to be set out on the fifty yard line."

"Good luck," one of the players said as I trotted toward the door. He slapped my shoulder. It was like getting whacked with an iron skillet. But it was cool.

"Hey, y'all, it's Rockin' Tony the Tiger." Tony's voice blasted through the locker room's sound system. "Get yourselves ready for some truly hard-core competition. Something that takes true physical ability."

"Hey!" yelled one of the players in mock

anger. At least I was hoping it was mock.

"You're about to see six young men go head to head. Or should I say stomach to stomach, in the final round of the Football Franks Hot Dog Eating Contest! Give it up!" Tony yelled. And the crowd roared in response.

For the first time it hit me—really hit me—that all those people in the packed stadium who'd been watching the game were going to be watching me in about a minute. The thought didn't do much for my stomach. All I could think was, please don't let me hurl on national television.

"First up, we've got Jordan Watnabe." Mr. Poplin opened the door for Jordan and he jogged out, waving to the crowd as they cheered for him.

"Now here's Vern Ricci!"

Vern shoved his bangs out of his face, then walked through the door.

"Next up, Kyle 'the Cannibal' Skloot!"

"See you out there, losers," Kyle said to the rest of us with a grin.

"Don't worry," Joe told me as Kyle ran out the door. "I came up with excellent eater names for us."

"What?" I demanded.

But Tony was already talking again, introducing Douglas to loud applause.

"Now we have a pair of cousins," Tony went on.

"We have Joe 'the Wood Chipper' Hardy," Tony cried.

"You put a cannibal in a wood chipper, one dead cannibal comes out the other side," Joe explained. Then he grinned and trotted out the door, doing the prize fighter handclasp over his head.

"And Frank 'the Vacuum Cleaner' Hardy!" Tony yelled out.

That's it? I thought as I ran out into the blazing Miami sunlight. *He gets to be a wood chipper and I get to be Aunt Trudy's favorite household appliance?*

I scowled at Joe as I sat down at the table between him and Jordan and across from Kyle. He gave me a wide-eyed what's-the-prob-bro look in response. As if he didn't know.

Tony started to give the rundown of the rules, as the piles, and piles, and piles of hot dogs were brought out and placed in front of us. I tuned out his voice. I knew all the rules by heart. Instead I concentrated on making sure I knew exactly where Kyle's hands were. Joe would be watching Douglas's. There was still time for one of them to try to add a little poison to the food we were about to shovel down. Or, in my case, I guess it should be vacuum up.

The cheerleaders right behind me were shouting. The crowd was shouting along with them.

Kyle's hands, I told myself. *That's all you care about. Kyle's hands*.

Then *bang!* The starter pistol went off. And all Kyle's hands were doing was getting the hot dogs from the plate to his gaping mouth. It was on.

I ripped the buns off ten hot dogs. Then I used both fists to crush the buns into balls as small as vitamins. I'd decided I liked this method better than dunking. I shoved all ten little bun vitamins into my mouth and swallowed them with the help of a swig of water.

Now the dogs. I wasn't crazy about the Solomon method. My throat still didn't feel two-conveyer-belt wide. But I hadn't found anything I liked better. I broke the first dog in half and put the pieces in my mouth side by side, then I raised my arms over my head and snaked my body back and forth. It wasn't a shimmy. It was more like a sway. But it got the dogs down with minimal chewing time.

I repeated the process. Break. Put the dogs on the belt. Sway/swallow. I tried not to think. About anything. Especially not how the dogs felt going down. They weren't bad once they were in my stomach. But if I thought about them on the way down, they immediately wanted to come back up. And that would get me eliminated.

Break. Put the dogs on the belt. Sway/swallow. I

was very, very glad when I could return to the bun removal and crushing portion of my routine.

The back of my neck started to perspire. Then my eyes started to sting as sweat ran into them. Meat sweats? Or just regular sweats from sitting in the sun? Didn't matter. I wasn't stopping now. No one was. I could see blurs of motion all around the table.

I was back to the dogs again. Break. Put the dogs on the belt. Sway/swallow. And repeat. *It's like what Joe said about shampooing your hair*, I thought wildly. *Lather, rinse, and repeat.*

"One minute, guys," Tony shouted. "One minute remaining."

Time to cram. I did one last sway/swallow. Then I started using my teeth to shred the dogs into tiny bits like I was a human, yeah, wood chipper. I shoved the bits into my cheeks, then did the lather, rinse, and repeat. My cheeks were bulging when Tony called time.

My counter leaned close and watched as I slowly, very slowly, managed to transfer all those hot dog bits from my cheeks to my throat to my belly. The cheerleaders gave it up for me as my counter added up all the hot dogs I'd eaten, making sure to check under the table to make sure none had ended up there instead of in my stomach.

I had no idea how many I'd eaten. It was like I'd

turned into a machine during the twenty minutes. A machine that couldn't do anything but eat. Not even something basic like count.

The counters gathered in a cluster with Tony and Mr. Poplin. "I'll spare you the stress of waiting," Kyle told us. "I won."

Joe rolled his eyes. "Wood chipper beats cannibal, dude," he muttered.

"And the winner is—" Tony made us wait for it, then gave it up. "Kyle Skloot!"

"Nothing beats the Cannibal," Kyle said with a smile.

Joe reached across the table and shook his hand. So did Jordan, Douglas, and I. Vern looked too ill to move.

"Kyle, come back to the locker room with me," Mr. Poplin said as he came up to the table. "We have a press conference set up." He smiled at the rest of us. "You boys did an amazing job. Enjoy the rest of the game."

"Have you heard anything about Angie?" I asked. It seemed less complicated not to admit we knew who she really was.

"Her parents are with her. Strange situation there . . ." Mr. Poplin let his words trail off, clearly wanting to keep the family's secrets. "But her condition is stable. She's going to be fine. The family's going to be fine. They're working everything out. I just wish I knew who did that to her. And I'm still thinking about that device on your surfboard, Jordan. They'd never seen anything like it at the surf shop."

Joe and I were still thinking about the device too. And the rattler. And the poison that had been put in Savannah's salad. And David's murder.

After the game, we'd all be heading back to the hotel to get our stuff, then we'd be going home. Our suspects would be flying off to different states. Joe and I were running out of time to solve this.

"We probably shouldn't keep the reporters waiting," said Kyle.

Mr. Poplin frowned but said, "Probably not. We'll be back in a bit," he added.

Jordan led the way back over to our amazing front-row seats. He didn't seem very upset over losing. Douglas looked pretty bummed, but not homicidal. It was hard to tell about Vern. He looked pale and sweaty and out of it, but that could be from eating all those dogs in such a short time. I was pretty sure I didn't look that good myself.

"Hey, Vern, you came in second!" Jordan called. He pointed to the blimp. He was right. Kyle had eaten sixty-three hot dogs. Vern had eaten sixty-two and a half.

"Oh, man, so close," Joe sympathized. "You did

great. The next competition you enter, I'm sure you're going to win."

"I'm not entering another one," Vern snapped just as Kyle's giant head appeared on all the screens around the stadium.

"Our hot dog eating champ, Kyle Skloot!" Tony cried over the sound system. "Tell us how you feel, Kyle."

"I feel awesome!" Kyle exclaimed. "Just the way I knew I'd feel. I've been visualizing this moment for months. That was one of my techniques. Visualizing how I'd feel when I triumphed. Hearing my victory applause. Seeing the faces of my defeated competitors."

"I think I'm going to be sick," Joe said. "And it has nothing to do with eating"—he checked his numbers on the blimp—"thirty-one hot dogs. Hey!" He turned to me. "You beat me. How could that happen. Wood chipper definitely beats vacuum."

I shook my head at him. "Have you forgotten? Older brother definitely beats younger brother."

"The game's about to start!" Jordan announced. "They're getting Kyle off the screen."

"But everybody watching the game on TV, which is more than a hundred and thirty-seven million, had to hear what he had to say," Vern told him.

"A hundred and thirty-seven million? Wow, I

knew it was a lot, but I didn't know it was that many," I answered as the teams ran back onto the field.

"Do you want to go to the bathroom, Vern?" Joe asked. "You're not looking too well."

It was true. Vern was looking even worse than before. His eyes were darting around feverishly. "I'm okay. Maybe I'll just have some of my aloe vera juice." He picked up the plastic jug and uncapped it, but managed to spill it before he got it to his mouth.

I grabbed some napkins out of my pocket and started to mop it up. I didn't want my feet to end up stuck to the ground. I might need to move fast at some point—if Joe and I did finally get a break in the case.

Vern crouched down next to me and helped. One of his shirtsleeves had gotten soaked, and he shoved it up. I didn't know why he was wearing long sleeves in Miami anyway.

I reached to get a place he'd missed, and that's when I saw it. A few inches above his wrist—two perfect puncture marks. A snakebite.

"Vern! Did that snake get you yesterday?" I burst out.

"No. I just . . . got a mosquito bite or something." Vern tried to jerk his sleeve back down. I grabbed his wrist to stop him.

"No way are those mosquito bites," I said. "They're too deep. And they're too perfectly placed. That's a snakebite. But it's not red or puffy."

"So there wasn't any poison in the rattler's fangs." Joe grabbed Vern by the other arm.

"What are you doing?" Jordan exclaimed. The crowd let out a howl, reacting to something on the field.

"Vern's the killer. That rattler was his. But he'd had the venom extracted," I shouted over the noise. The facts were clicking into place almost too fast to process.

"That's why you always had the Do Not Disturb sign on your door," cried Joe. "You didn't want one of the cleaning people to find the snake before you were ready to stage your attack on yourself!"

"An attack that would throw suspicion off of you," I added. "Come on. We're taking you to security."

Vern wrenched free. He ran in the only direction open to him—straight onto the field. Straight into the rush of charging bodies. Massive charging bodies.

14.
Dead Meat

A referee was immediately after Vern. But Frank and I couldn't chance him getting away. We plunged onto the field ourselves.

The players were so intent on the game they hadn't noticed the interruption. I dodged left, but still managed to take a hit on my right side that sent me sprawling into the mix of grass and mud.

Cleats came pounding toward me. I covered my head with my hands and rolled. Then I was up again.

The game had staggered to a halt, but Vern was still running. The ref was still after him, and Frank and I had both picked up referee tails too. I put on as much speed as I could, my right knee begging me to just sit down.

148

Vern was so close. I could almost reach him. "Get him, Joe!" Frank yelled.

So I went low and rammed my shoulder into the back of Vern's knees. And I was down again. But so was Vern.

A second later we were both surrounded by refs, players, and cameras. Lots and lots of cameras. Out of the corner of my eye, I could see Vern and me up on the huge stadium screens.

"I have a message," Vern screamed, turning toward the biggest cluster of cameras. "I have a message for America. For all you millions of people who were just entertained by the sight of people shoving meat into their faces. Meat is murder!"

Refs began to "escort" me, Frank, and Vern off the field. Vern dug his feet into the grass, making them work to move him. He kept screaming the whole time. "Do you know how much suffering goes into every hot dog? Every hamburger? Every chicken wing? The torture must stop! The murder must stop!"

The crowd went insane as we were hauled into the Cowboys' locker room. Well, Vern was hauled. Frank and I walked. Most of them booed. But a few gave up cheers for Vern and his message.

We didn't have to worry about getting Vern to

the police. There were police right there in the locker room waiting for us. In case you're wondering, running onto the field during the Super Bowl is illegal.

But not nearly as illegal as killing people. Frank and I convinced the police to check out Vern's hotel room. There was evidence a rattler had been kept in a cage in the closet. There was also a planter of elephant ear in the bathroom. And a backup of the device that had made the shark go after Jordan's board.

After they found all that, the police decided to let me and Frank go and concentrate on Vern's crimes. "So the murder and murder attempts really were about hot dogs, in a weird way," I said to Frank as we packed up our stuff.

"The evilness of hot dogs," Frank agreed. "Vern knew if he won the contest, he'd get on TV in front of all the people watching the Super Bowl. That's all he wanted. Airtime to tell everyone meat is murder."

"He didn't seem to care that much that murder is murder too," I commented.

"Now, I expect you boys to eat properly," Aunt Trudy said as she placed the lasagna on the table and sat down with the rest of the family. "I can't tell you how embarrassed I was by your manners when I saw you on television."

"We had to enter the contest. It was part of the deal when I won the tickets on the radio. And picnic rules weren't in place," I told her.

"I don't know or care what that means," she said.

"Picnic rules don't allow for taking food apart or crushing it or dunking it in water during an eating competition," Mom explained.

"Is there anything you don't know?" Frank asked her.

I don't know how he can be surprised at this point. Mom's a research librarian, and she can come up with facts about pretty much any subject off the top of her head.

"No matter what the rules are, it's still disgusting, and it looked as if you just weren't raised right," Aunt Trudy complained.

"Some people think of it as a sport, Aunt T," I told her. "Just like football or anything else. It takes training, endurance—"

"Dumbheadedness," Aunt Trudy cut me off. "And you know what's even more dumbheadedness, those Vern Ferns."

"I saw something more about them on the news this morning," said Dad. "It's amazing how fast a fan club formed for that boy."

"That boy who's a murderer," Aunt Trudy shot back.

"His message about the way animals are treated before slaughter clearly made a big impression on some people," Mom commented.

It was true. People were already wearing T-shirts and buttons with MEAT IS MURDER printed on them. Vern had gotten his message out there. And he'd sacrificed a lot to do it. He'd eaten meat, something he thought was deeply immoral. And he'd prepared it. We'd found out he was one of the cooks for the competition where David died.

Frank took a small bite of lasagna. Aunt Trudy smiled at him approvingly. I shook my head. "I still can't believe you beat me in an eating contest. Everyone knows I'm the best eater in the family," I said.

"I'm not surprised," Mom told me.

"How can you say that?" I demanded. "When I'm your favorite!"

She smiled at me. "I love you both the same. But I'm not at all surprised he beat you, and I deserve all the credit."

"Why you? He's my son too," said Dad.

"True," she answered. "But I'm the one who named him Frank."

It's a good thing bad jokes can't kill you, or Mom would have just taken out the entire Hardy family.